THE THREE SISTERS TRILOGY BOOK 1

THE TANGLEWOOD WITCHES

USA TODAY BESTSELLING AUTHOR

GENEVIEVE JACK

PART I
TANGLEWOOD ORIGINS

CHAPTER ONE

Alexandria, Egypt, 30 BC

"Unhand me. I demand to know what this is about!" Alena grunted as the guard's palm rudely connected with the center of her back and thrust her into the stone cell with no regard for her ongoing protests.

This morning had gone from bad to worse. At the crack of dawn, a team of Egyptian soldiers had hauled her out of her meager lodgings and dragged her to Cleopatra's palace. The soldiers had offered no explanation for her arrest. That was bad.

But if the experience had warranted the label of worst day since she'd come to Egypt, her current situation trumped that epithet. She found herself in a crowded room that smelled of limestone and dark spices, and judging by her company, the guards had made a terrible mistake.

She rubbed her sleepy eyes and took in the others around her. It wasn't just her tattered, filthy garments that made her stand out like Zeus's lightning bolt; she was the only woman in the group, and based on appearances, these men were important. *Sau* priests if the leopard skins draped over their shoulders was any indication. Powerful magicians. Each was completely shaven of all body hair, as was the custom. Dressed in light linen, they sparkled from their bald heads to their bare toenails. She'd never been that clean in her life.

Suddenly she realized the source of the scent she'd noticed when she arrived. Not dark spices but anointing oils. The priests gave her a disapproving look, and she moved away from them to huddle on the far side of the room.

She did not belong here. Not only was she not a priest, she wasn't even Egyptian. Alena hailed from Crete, Greece, a commoner who had taken to the healing arts. She'd only made the perilous journey to Egypt to study in the library of Alexandria. Herbs and pharmacopoeia were her passion, and she wished to learn what knowledge the books and scrolls there contained. The library had almost burned down once. It was her life's dream to investigate what it had to offer before some other disaster challenged its stacks.

Her father had begged her not to go. He'd become dependent on her in many ways, the least of which was to fill the hole that had been left when her mother died. But two seasons ago she'd realized she would never leave Crete or realize her potential as a healer if she didn't seek passage to the greatest source of knowledge her generation had ever known.

Thank the gods her talents had proven lucrative. Quickly she had taken to tending the sick and acting as a midwife. News of her competence had traveled far and wide and earned her the sobriquet of Healer of the Nile. And although it was dirty work and she was rarely paid in coin, her calling had provided a suitable dwelling and a full belly.

At least the presence of the priests in this stone room meant she wasn't in any real danger. Why would Cleopatra imprison her own sorcerers? This was either a misunderstanding or some sort of royal request for services. Perhaps the pharaoh was in need of healing. She tried to remain calm and take comfort in the fact that she was in the company of important men, not criminals.

"Well, well, well. If it isn't the Healer of the Nile," a man said from behind her.

Her spine stiffened. She knew that voice. She hated that voice. She closed her eyes and sighed before turning to face him.

"Orpheus, the louse charmer." She shot the man a slanted glance. Like her, Orpheus stood out from the others in the room, although his clothing was also of far better quality than hers. His thick black hair and short beard contradicted the clean-shaven heads of the others, and he was certainly *not* a priest. A smooth-talking charlatan maybe, but not a priest.

By profession, he was a popular barber, one who claimed the rare distinction of successfully ridding heads of vermin without having to shave them. The skill was all but unheard of, and people came from everywhere for his services. Truly, it was a shame a man of such talent and wealth had the personality of a pimple on the ass of a diseased rat.

"Why the hostility, Alena? You're not still mad about what happened between us?" He flashed his most disarming smile.

She silently cursed as her insides reacted with a reflexive rush of lightning. The man was devastatingly handsome with the tawny glow of one blessed by the gods. In other circumstances, she would feel quite honored to have garnered his attention, she'd give him that. Dark-haired and blue-eyed, he had a mouth that seemed locked in a permanent smirk. She'd made the mistake of kissing that mouth, an act akin to drinking sweet poison.

An exasperated sigh tore from her lips. "Did *you* have something to do with this? You did something stupid, didn't you, and then likely threw out *my* name as an alibi!"

"No!" He scoffed.

She spread her hands and gestured toward the priests, who were doing their best to ignore them properly. "Then why are *we* here?"

"No idea, but we are the only ones in this room not employed by Cleopatra. These men are magicians, sorcerers, priests. They tend to the gods. It seems odd they've summoned us as well."

"My thoughts exactly." Alena hated to agree with Orpheus about anything, but she was hard-pressed to come up with any explanation.

Their conversation was interrupted by the heavy grinding of stone on stone. Alena whirled to find soldiers sliding a heavy slab into the doorway, completely sealing off the exit. With no windows or alternate ways out of the tiny room, Alena instantly felt choked off.

"Stop! What are you doing?" She lurched toward the door, but Orpheus caught her by the arms.

"Those swords aren't for show, Alena. Whatever they have in store for us, you won't avoid it that way."

"But... but... we're trapped in here." Pain flared in her chest, and her breath came in ragged pants.

"Easy." Orpheus rubbed her shoulders. Her wild eyes found his and he guided her through some deep breaths. "Keep your wits about you. We're going to need them."

Slowly her panic abated. Despite being a rake and a

scoundrel, Orpheus was an important man in Alexandria. Surely she was safe here among the priests and him. A half dozen torches mounted above their heads bathed them in flickering shadows.

"I can't even make out the door we came through," Alena said.

"Odd that." Orpheus grimaced, showing a mouthful of suspiciously straight white teeth. No other man, Greek or Egyptian, sported such a perfect smile. She wondered for the hundredth time what bargain he'd struck with the gods to maintain his impossibly good looks.

"Can't you charm a louse to squeeze through the walls and get us out of here?" Alena said through her teeth, annoyed by his nearness. She crossed her arms between them and tapped her foot expectantly in his direction.

"If there was a louse among this hairless crew, yes I could."

"I have hair."

He arched a brow. "And we both know that thanks to your herbal concoctions, there isn't a single louse on you either. Although what a tiny insect could do to open a stone door anyway, I have no idea. Unfortunately, there isn't a single living thing in this room that would be any help in getting us out of it."

She shook her head. "As expected, a bastion of self-importance but completely useless in a crunch."

He recoiled from the insult but recovered soon enough. "What about you, Alena? Don't you have anything in that bag that could help us?" He glared at the satchel at her hip.

She didn't go anywhere without her apothecary basket, and she'd felt fortunate when the guards had allowed her to bring it. Inside, she stored a wide variety of herbs and elixirs in small glass jars or wrapped in parchment.

She placed a protective hand over it. "Only if we all come down with fever."

Nonchalantly, he leaned a shoulder against the wall and crossed his legs at the ankle. "As expected. Asserts to raise the dead but completely useless in an emergency."

"I never said I could raise the dead! Oh, you're a child." She turned her back to him, a welcome surge of anger and frustration driving out her previous fears.

"Frankly, I'm surprised the soldiers allowed you to bring your apothecary," he murmured thoughtfully.

She turned back to him. "It was unusual. At the time, I assumed someone in the palace needed healing, but clearly that's not why I'm here." Her eyes narrowed on him.

"Why are *you* here anyway? Didn't you tell Cleopatra's guards that you're an archon of Athens, invited here as an advisor by the pharaoh herself?"

His face fell at her reference to the lie he'd used to try to take advantage of her. "I never said I was an archon. You assumed."

She clenched her teeth. "Only because you had suggested as much on the boat to Alexandria. The elaborate clothing, the food, the servants. It all seemed to indicate you were an important government official, a leader."

"As I recall, you benefited frequently from my generosity."

She couldn't deny it. He had been generous, and at the time that generosity had meant everything to her.

"The crew of the vessel said you were the eponymous archon of Athens. Who would have told them such if not you? And you did not refute it, although you must have heard the rumors."

"Is it my duty to correct every wagging tongue? Athens

has a council of archons, not a single magistrate. You should have known it was a falsehood."

"You knew and you allowed me to believe it. It was under that presumption that I allowed you to woo me within a hair's breadth of your bed, only to discover in the most embarrassing way that it was all a lie."

For weeks he'd pursued her, bringing her gifts, sharing long walks, even doing his best to bump into her at the market. But then he'd invited her to a feast at the home of a prominent Alexandrian. It was there that a group of elderly wives had pulled her aside and told her the truth. He was the louse charmer—their name for the barber—and she was one of many women he'd wooed under false pretenses. He was a cad, a rake, and a scoundrel. The old women had wasted no time sharing their deep regret that her reputation among the elite was already scarred by arriving on his arm.

"I pursued you because I enjoyed your company." He gave her a wicked half smile. "Not only to bed you."

"He flirts with every woman in the city," she said, mimicking the voice of the old women. "He's a scoundrel, a cheater. Allow him between your legs and it will be the last time he gives you any attention whatsoever."

"Untrue. You can't believe such things." He raised an eyebrow.

"Oh?" She planted her fists on her hips. "And the woman I saw coming out of your abode on the last moon?"

He opened his mouth but stopped short. His gaze lifted toward the ceiling. "Not that I don't love debating the history of our meeting and my scandalous behavior once again, but does it appear to you that the smoke is gathering?"

Alena glanced upward to find a thick cloud building above them. "The torches. There's no ventilation." The small, windowless room was growing warmer as well.

Already her eyes stung, and the air appeared cloudy between them. "There isn't enough space and too many mouths breathing. Orpheus, if this keeps building..." She gave him an ominous look.

He inhaled deeply and muttered something inaudible under his breath.

One of the priests tested the door. As she suspected, it was sealed. Alena couldn't even see the outline of the opening in the stone. Another priest pounded on the walls and cried for help. Still another tried to scale the wall to put out one of the torches, but the brace was set too high and caged in iron. Worse, Alena noticed more smoke coming through the stone up above.

"They're doing this on purpose!" she cried, gathering a loose bit of fabric from the neck of her cloak and pressing it around her mouth and nose. Did Cleopatra mean to kill them all?

The smoke thickened by the minute. The walls were too close, the air too tight. True fear pulverized her resolve to stay calm, and the shaking in her knees spread to the rest of her body. Orpheus tugged on her hand, gesturing for her to sit. Considering her knees were about to give out anyway, she dropped to the rough, mercifully cool floor. The air was cleaner there, and she drew in a panicked breath.

"Alena, it's a test," Orpheus said with utmost certainty.

She stared at him with stinging eyes, willing her addled brain to understand what he was talking about. To her surprise, he didn't seem to be struggling to breathe at all. Nor was he panicked as she was.

"What kind of test?" she rasped. "One to see who can hold their breath the longest? I fear we will all fail. Cleopatra may be the reincarnation of Isis, but the rest of us are only human."

"Are you?" Orpheus's eyes crinkled at the corners.

"Aren't *you*?" Alena's gaze connected with his through the smoky air.

One of the priests banged on the wall in earnest now, his pleas for release growing as he struggled for air, while still others slumped or crawled on their bellies, anything for a small measure of comfort. She lowered her chest to the floor. Orpheus followed, although the smoke didn't seem to be bothering him anyway.

"Haven't you noticed that everyone in this room has a reputation for magic?" he asked.

"Not everyone. I do not advertise myself as such." She coughed into her cloak.

"Ah, but it is known, Alena. You are the healer they say can make a tonic to cure any ill. Some call you a hedge witch."

She coughed violently. "Those who wish to be healed should stop making up names for me."

"But they aren't wrong, are they?"

A priest who'd balanced on the shoulders of another to try to extinguish one of the torches fell unconscious to the stone floor. His head cracked near her hand. Blood ran from his fractured skull, scoring a deep crimson river in the stone. Alena shuffled away from it. Her instinct was to dig in her basket and find something to try to heal him, but she could hardly breathe herself. They were all doomed. All but Orpheus, who hadn't coughed once.

"You believe this is a test of our abilities? Someone is trying to prove we have... magic?"

His lips pursed and he gave a curt nod. "It would be a particularly gruesome horror to watch a woman as beautiful as you die. I'd much prefer your company under sweeter circumstances. I enjoyed our time together up until those crones ruined everything with their lies. More than I can say." He grabbed her arm and gave her a hard shake. "Come on, Alena. Think. Tell me you have something in that bag you can use. How hard can it be? All you have to do is survive."

Her throat and eyes burned and her lungs spasmed with their need for air. She cursed. Why wasn't he as affected as she? He still wasn't coughing, and his eyes glowed an arresting shade of lapis in the dingy room. She shook her head and concentrated. He was right. She was a powerful healer. There must be something she could use to protect herself from the smoke if she could calm herself long enough to remember how to use it. Digging in her basket, she drew a length of aeras lily root and wove a braid of Nile grasses around it. Muttering a spell, she formed the resulting mask into a shallow bowl and cupped it over her mouth and nose. Instantly, she could breathe again.

"Aeras root. I hadn't thought of that."

"I developed this spell for a boy in the village who has trouble breathing during the dry season. I wouldn't have thought to use it if you hadn't..." She stopped. She wouldn't give him the satisfaction. "What did you use?"

"Containment spell. I'm inside a sophisticated barrier. Although, to be honest, I didn't think it through. The air is getting thin in here. If this test goes on much longer, I may be joining our friends." He gestured to the priests who were now writhing on the floor, either coughing or limp and unconscious. "I can't renew the spell without any fresh air to seal around myself."

Alena could see it now, how the smoke never seemed to actually touch Orpheus. It curled away from his flesh. Genius, she thought. She'd love to ask him about that particular spell if they ever got out of this room.

"How long have you known about me?" she asked.

"Since the feast. When I kissed you, I knew you were magic. Couldn't you sense it in me?"

She searched his face. The kiss had sent tingles through her body, but it wasn't as though she'd had anything to compare it to. Weren't all kisses like that? She shook her head.

Orpheus shrugged and started to cough. "Hades, it seems my spell is wearing off. And no closer to finding out what Cleopatra wants from us, other than to die."

No one could claim to know the mind of Cleopatra. Far above the commoners of Egypt, her will was a maze of secrets known only to her. Alena had always thought it would be lonely to be a pharaoh; perhaps that was why it wasn't hard to believe the rumors that Cleopatra's obsessive quest for power had made her a killer. Some said she'd murdered her own brother for the throne.

Orpheus pressed his face into his hands, body stretched out on the floor. She had to make a difficult decision. Did she assume this trial must have one winner and allow the smoke to overcome him? Or did she help him and risk inviting the wrath of Cleopatra?

In the end, there was no decision to make. It was bad enough to live with the knowledge that she could do nothing to help the other men who'd collapsed in the room. Refusing aid to Orpheus when he was the reason she'd thought to build the mask in the first place would be a black mark on her soul she could not abide.

Alena took a deep breath and then moved her mask to cover Orpheus's nose and mouth. His body eased beside her, his breathing evening out. He took three long breaths, then moved the mask back to her face. They survived together, sharing the mask, until the smoke was so thick she could no longer see the walls of the room, only his deep-blue eyes.

And then the stone-on-stone rumble filled the room again. Not the door this time. Like a dream, one entire wall of their cell slid away. Cool air wafted around them. The smoke rose up and out in a billow of gray. Light cut through the foggy air. Orpheus had her by the shoulders and was helping her to her feet.

She blinked rapidly. Through the dispelling haze, she could make out a vast hall ahead of them with brightly painted columns. Colorful tapestries draped the walls, and a long red rug led to a dais. She squinted to make out who or what was on that platform at the other end of the room, but her eyes still stung from the smoke, and their watering blurred her vision. Alena leaned into Orpheus, and together they hobbled along the aisle. Fire burned in a series of great gold bowls lighting their way. Alena blinked and blinked again.

Dread filled her heart when she realized who it was on that platform, sitting on her golden throne. Not some soldier or priest or counselor as she'd expected but Cleopatra herself.

Her hair was as black and shiny as the Nile at midnight, and her clothing was solid gold. Everything about her was fashioned to intimidate her subjects, from the robe made to resemble the feathers of Isis to the headdress of horns that framed a large red disk that reflected the light of the flickering torches in a way that seemed supernatural.

Alena swallowed hard. This woman ruled Egypt. She truly might be a goddess for all Alena knew. She definitely held their lives in her hands. It was said she was beautiful, but Alena didn't see beauty, only power. She radiated it like a deadly, burning sun.

Orpheus tugged her shoulders as they arrived at the base of the dais, and she followed his lead, dropping to her knees beside him.

An elderly man who stood beside the pharaoh announced, "All hail Cleopatra, the embodiment of Isis, sister to Horus and Ra, and queen of all Egypt."

Alena lowered her forehead to the floor and prayed to all the gods whose names she could remember that the worst was already behind her.

CHAPTER TWO

"Rise," Cleopatra commanded.

Orpheus climbed to his feet and helped Alena to hers. She seemed rightfully flustered, and he steadied her with a firm hand on her shoulder. Everything about this situation made him uneasy. It was well known that Cleopatra had become unhinged in recent years. On a whim, she could have both of them beheaded and spend the rest of the afternoon kicking their skulls around her throne room for sport. Her power was ultimate.

Alena had saved his life. She must feel something for him despite what had happened between them. Though this was not how he'd thought things would proceed. *He* should be saving *her* if he was ever going to make up for what he'd done to her. It was rotten luck that he'd needed rescuing. His spell should have been sufficient. But all magic was unpredictable, especially here in the palace where it was said the gods were closest to the realm of man.

"Two. Only two worthy sorcerers in all my lands," Cleopatra snapped. Her blood-colored nails dug into the arms of her throne as she scowled at the pile of bodies still in the stone room at the other end of the enormous hall. "So be it. You will be my champions."

Orpheus fisted his hands to keep from saying something he might regret. Years ago, he'd heard that Cleopatra had rolled herself inside a carpet and had it delivered to Julius Caesar in order to orchestrate a meeting with the emperor. A cunning move. That relationship had resulted in a son, a son whose father had been murdered. Now the queen was married to Mark Antony, although he was away fighting her battles. People around Cleopatra tended to die. Her merciless rule was characterized by a great many more horrors than a few dead priests.

It was all made worse by his desire to protect Alena. She was a powerful healer, but she had the gentlest soul he'd ever come across. He'd spent months chastising himself over the lie of omission. Those aristocratic women had treated her cruelly with their nasty gossip and outright rejection of her. Alena had been the source of the most exciting kiss he'd ever experienced, and he was painfully aware that, underneath her tattered cloak, she had the heart of an angel. Several other interesting things probably existed beneath that cloak as well. Things he should very much like to explore in the future if he survived this day.

He took a fortifying breath and tried to think about what his father would do in this situation. The man could usually talk his way out of anything.

"How can I be of service to you, my queen?" he said lightly. He bowed low, his stomach churning at the thought of carrying out any appalling request the ruler might make.

Cleopatra drummed her fingers on the arm of her throne. "You are Orpheus, the barber?"

"Yes." Out of the corner of his eye, he noticed Alena's head turn, and her perusal burned against his cheek.

"And you..." Cleopatra turned her full attention on Alena. "They call you a hedge witch, the Healer of the Nile."

Alena's throat bobbed. "An exaggeration. I have an affinity for plants and herbs and their many uses."

"I have been told by a reliable source that you brought a man's goat back from the dead."

"I only kept it from dying."

"Are you saying my source is a liar?"

Orpheus cringed. He could see Alena growing flustered. Didn't she realize that downplaying her gifts would only hurt her situation? They'd survived Cleopatra's test. The pharaoh would not believe her denial of power now.

"Perhaps the man only thought the goat was dead," he offered.

Alena blinked rapidly. "That's right. Your source isn't lying; he simply wasn't near enough to see what I saw. The goat was still alive. I gave it a tonic, and it revived. That is all."

Cleopatra lifted her chin. "A barber and a simple healer." She stared down her nose at them from her throne. "Still, you survived my test when my most powerful priests did not. There may be hope for you yet."

"I was fortunate to have my bag of pharmacopoeia with me." Alena tapped the large satchel at her hip.

"And you shall have it when you take up my quest."

Orpheus's face turned cold, as if all the blood had drained from it, and his heart fluttered. So this wasn't over. "What is this quest you speak of, my queen?"

"Octavian's legions even now are invading Egypt. Our armies are outmatched." Cleopatra paused for a long while, then spoke in a low voice as if she did not want the gods to hear. "What you do not know is that Mark Antony is gravely injured."

Alena gasped, covering her mouth with her hand.

"Calm yourself, hedge witch. I shall set things right if you and the barber succeed. I need you to retrieve something for me, a book of magic with equal ability to heal as well as destroy. A golden grimoire, promised to me by the gods."

Orpheus exchanged glances with Alena, who looked as confused as he felt. He cleared his throat. "Where do we find this grimoire?"

"Follow me." Cleopatra rose from her throne, her golden robes clinking with her movement. Snapping her fingers, she called a large, heavily armed guard to her side. "Make sure they behave, Ledmur."

The guard followed behind them menacingly as the pharaoh led them deeper into the palace, the stone passageways narrowing with their progress. Orpheus glanced back when Alena grabbed his hand and squeezed. He could guess what she was thinking. It was highly unusual to be alone like this with the queen, even with an armed guard. And for her to share the news of Mark Antony's fatal injuries meant she did not fear they would ever have the chance to speak that secret to anyone else anytime soon.

"My palace has many hidden passageways," she said, the torchlight reflecting in her dark eyes.

She unlocked an ordinary door and led them into an even narrower corridor, barely wider than Orpheus's shoulders. Alena kept hold of his hand as she followed behind him.

"I've explored every one. Doors upon doors. But this one, this door revealed itself only days ago, the day I prayed for a way to avenge Mark Antony."

The passage opened into a dark, cavernous room with rough-hewn walls where torches flickered and shadows danced. Orpheus glanced at Alena, who'd moved closer to his side. Her lips parted as she took in the massive golden carvings before them. Orpheus was just as dumbstruck. The ancient symbols meant nothing to him, but at the center of the closed doors was the unmistakable shape of a gold peacock.

"The gods have heard my prayers. The peacock, you see, is a symbol of the all-knowing Eye of Horus. He sees and he has sent me this." She pointed to a series of inscriptions in the stone, which Orpheus couldn't read. It wasn't Greek or Egyptian. "This writing is in an ancient language only one of my high priests could translate. It says the grimoire is protected by a series of challenges meant to keep the unworthy from possessing it. It tells of the book's power to heal and destroy our enemies." Cleopatra's fingers trailed over the symbols. "Unfortunately, none of my champions have been able to retrieve it."

"Is the door charmed?" Alena asked.

Cleopatra laughed. "No. It will open for you. Entering is not the problem. Coming out alive is."

Orpheus swallowed and felt Alena shiver. "Others have attempted this quest?"

Cleopatra's kohl-rimmed eyes met his. "None have succeeded."

"How do you expect *us* to survive if the door has only ever led to death?" Alena protested in a trembling voice.

The queen tilted her head. "You survived my trial, hedge witch. Use your powers. This challenge should be easy for you and the barber. Simply follow the path to its end."

"And if we refuse?" Orpheus scowled.

"There is no way out of this room without the grimoire." Her blood-red lips formed an exaggerated pout.

The guard drew his sword. Orpheus could try magic, but

he was sure there would be more guards. They were outnumbered here.

He glanced again toward Alena, whose expression bordered on panic. "I don't suppose we have an option."

Cleopatra gave him a patronizing look. "No."

"The golden door or certain death," Alena murmured.

"Every day without the weapon is a day we risk defeat against Octavian's legions. Take heart, barber. The gods brought us this door. If your hearts are pure, surely the gods will come to your aid."

"My heart hasn't been pure since before the pyramids, my queen," he said sarcastically.

Cleopatra raised her chin. "Then you'd better hope hers is, for both your sakes. Now, I tire of your insolence." She gestured toward the door.

Orpheus focused on Alena. She was trembling. How he hated this, hated Cleopatra with every fiber of his being.

He offered Alena his hand. "How hard can it be? All we have to do is survive."

CHAPTER THREE

S urvive. Alena shook her head. Who knew what they were walking into? Anything gifted by the gods would also be protected by them, and all deities could be downright cruel in their games. Still, there was no choice. That was clear.

Against her better judgment, Alena slipped her hand into Orpheus's again and allowed him to guide her to the golden doors. Part of her hated relying on him for comfort, but a larger part was too terrified to deny herself the human contact. If she was going to die, she'd like to be holding on to someone when it happened. Even if that person was an unnerving but woefully attractive charlatan.

Did Cleopatra know what was on the other side? What had her previous champions described? Had Alena been braver, she might have asked. But at the moment, her tongue had turned to leather in her mouth, and she was clutching her basket to her stomach as hard as she was clutching Orpheus's fingers—as if her life depended on it. As if either could protect her from a test of the gods.

Together, they pushed against the doors.

White light flooded over them, and without taking a single step, Alena found she was standing inside a forest. Bleached white branches littered the ground, covered in dirt and leaves. She whirled and found the door closed behind her, its ornate gold panels surrounded by nothing but air as if they'd sprouted directly from the soil.

"That's a bad sign," Orpheus said.

"What?"

He pointed at the forest floor.

"The fallen branches?"

He laughed through his nose and arched a brow at her. "Those are bones, Alena, and I'm guessing that whatever picked them clean is close by."

The back of her neck prickled. Everything here was strange. The sky gave off a metallic glint. She could find no sun or moon, but a bright ambient light with no point of origination lit their way. The air was heavy and close. She scanned their surroundings: trees... bones... fallen leaves.

"There's a path," she whispered, pointing to a dirt rut that led deeper into the forest. "Perhaps if we are quiet, we can sneak past whatever it is and move beyond its territory."

He swallowed and nodded.

What other choice was there than to keep moving forward? With one eye on the strangely silver sky, she led the way, still holding Orpheus's hand. Her palms were sweaty now, and she was tempted to release him and wipe them on her cloak, but the idea of letting go of the comfort of his touch kept her clinging on.

They'd traveled deep enough into the woods that Alena was beginning to believe they might actually avoid whatever monster lived there when the thump of heavy wings beating the air reached her ears. A beast the likes of which Alena had only read about landed on the path in front of them, daggerlike claws dimpling the dirt. The dreadful creature had the body of a lion, a wingspan twice as long as she was tall, and the head of an extremely ugly man. She gasped and collided with Orpheus's side. He swept her behind him.

"A sphinx," he whispered to her. "Let me handle this."

The sphinx's bulbous nose wrinkled, and it bared its yellow teeth. "Ah, young lovers. Sweet meat."

"Oh, we're not lovers," Alena reflexively said, popping her head out from behind Orpheus.

Orpheus narrowed his eyes at her. "Truly? Is that important to share right now?"

She lowered her eyes, her cheeks burning.

"Your bones grind just as well." The sphinx flashed a grotesque grin.

"Allow us to pass," Orpheus boomed. "By order of Cleopatra."

The sphinx snorted, and a bit of snot rained onto the ground near its claws. "I care not what the human queen commands. You will solve my riddle, or you will not pass."

Alena nudged Orpheus's side. Her mother used to give her riddles to keep her occupied when she was young. "Riddles? I'm gifted at riddles. Always loved them as a child. I can do this."

"Quiet," he hissed. "Trust me."

Alena straightened and stepped out from behind Orpheus. No way was she going to let this... this... louse charmer get them killed. She could do this. She knew she could.

"That's it?" she said loudly. "All I have to do is solve your riddle? Give it to me then."

Orpheus tugged on her elbow. "What are you doing? You never ask a sphinx for its riddle!"

"Why not? I told you I'm very good at riddles. There

hasn't been one yet I couldn't solve." Alena faced the creature head-on and readied her mind.

The sphinx cleared its beastly throat and began to speak. "My death is never mourned, my work, taken for granted. My legacy is vast. For hundreds of years I've toiled beneath the sun, yet I have never done anything at all. I am a provider and a thief. I grow, I change, but I am always in the same place. What am I?"

Orpheus groaned. "That's impossible."

"No!" Alena slapped her hand over his mouth, but it was too late.

"Your answer is incorrect." The sphinx growled and lunged for them.

Alena braced herself to be torn apart, releasing her hold on Orpheus and crossing her arms to shield her face. But the attack never came. Instead, an enchanting and sweet melody met Alena's ears. She'd never before heard a more engaging tune. She could almost feel the music brushing past her like a living thing. Lowering her arms, she saw that Orpheus was singing. Before she understood what was happening, he'd grabbed her waist, swept her in a wide arc around the sphinx, and was ushering her along the path. The beast howled wildly but didn't seem capable of pursuing them.

"What? What's happening?"

Orpheus didn't answer. He dragged her down the path at a run, still singing like his life depended on it. He didn't stop running until they'd reached a bright green glade beside a winding stream. Not a hint of bones littered the ground here. He dropped his hold on her and ended his impromptu aria.

Resting his hands on his knees, he gasped for breath.

"Zeus, I am not a fan of singing while running at the same time. Let us not practice it again."

Alena placed her hands on her hips. "No. Let's not. Next time listen to me and follow my instructions and you won't have to."

"Hmm?" He glanced at her in confusion.

"If you hadn't been such an idiot and answered the riddle incorrectly, we wouldn't have had to run."

"Incorrectly? I never answered at all."

She rolled her eyes. "You said it was impossible. That counted as your answer. Haven't you studied anything about the sphinx? You only get one chance."

"*Humph*. We would never have figured it out anyway."

"The answer was a *tree*." She crossed her arms and popped out a hip.

"A tree?"

"'My death is never mourned.' Trees in the northern parts of the world die in the winter. They are not mourned because they come back to life in the spring."

"How do you know that?"

"I read." She shook her head. "'My work, taken for granted.' Trees provide living quarters for animals and lumber for homes and fires, but we never thank them. 'My legacy is vast.' Trees give off thousands of seeds. 'For hundreds of years I've toiled beneath the sun, yet I have never done anything at all. I grow, I change, but I am always in the same place.' This obviously refers to the tree being unable to move independently."

Orpheus's mouth dropped open. "What about the part referring to a provider and a thief?"

She sighed. "Trees provide lumber, shade, and fruit, but they steal water and nutrients from the earth. Honestly,

Orpheus." She closed her eyes and gave her head a disappointed shake.

He leaned back and stared at the sky. "Hmm. A tree. Yes, of course it is. It's so obvious now."

"Next time let me solve the riddles."

He waved a dismissive hand. "The sphinx would have likely eaten us anyway."

She gave him a stern look. "Which brings me to my next question: How did you stop it from eating us at all? What sort of sorcery was that?"

The man rolled his neck on his shoulders and shot her a serious look. "You don't believe it was a simple barber's trick?"

"Not a chance. It was magic, as was the spell that kept you alive in the stone room."

"*You* kept me alive in the stone room," he said seriously.

"You owe me an explanation. How is it you can perform magic? I'm beginning to think you aren't a common barber at all."

He sauntered closer to her, his gaze boring into hers. The smirk she thought might never leave his face morphed into a rare and serious expression. "*I* am beginning to think you are not so simple as to settle for a simple answer."

CHAPTER FOUR

O rpheus rubbed his neck and glanced away, avoiding the weight of Alena's rapt attention. He didn't like sharing his secret. If it got out who he really was, he'd never hear the end of it. People would swarm him, maybe even hurt him, to get what they wanted. He'd traveled a long way, posed as someone he wasn't, and chosen a frequently overlooked profession for the express purpose of avoiding attention. But what purpose did keeping his secret serve now, when the likelihood was he'd never make it out of here alive?

"The reason the crew called me an archon is that they heard my father say I was abusing the power gifted to me by the gods. They misinterpreted that as legislative power."

She narrowed her eyes. "What other interpretation is there?"

"My father is a wealthy Athenian merchant with an uncanny gift for negotiation. One might even say he has a silver tongue. Power of voice runs in our family."

Alena took a seat on a boulder near the stream and leaned toward him. "Go on."

"This special ability runs in our family because he is the son of Theneus, who is the son of Kaleus, who is a descendant of Cimon, son of Medus."

"Medus. *The* Medus?"

"The one of legend. Son of Medea and King Aegeus."

Her face paled. "Are you telling me that you are a descendant of the sorceress Medea and the goat-head king Aegeus?"

"I inherited my magic from Medea. I'm a fair sorcerer, but my greatest strength is that I can influence living things with my voice. As for the sphinx, I was able to convince it through song that it couldn't use its legs."

Alena pursed her lips.

"You don't believe me, do you?"

"You spend your days delousing people. Why would you do that if you were powerful enough to control any beast? You could be wealthy beyond your wildest dreams."

"I was already rich when I left Athens. I'd worked for my father for years and made a fortune. Besides, there's good money in delousing. I don't think you realize how lucrative it is."

She stared at him incredulously.

"Why don't *you* tell everyone what you are?" he countered. "I know you raised that goat from the dead. You're far more powerful than an ordinary healer."

For a long moment, Alena took an interest in the babbling brook winding through the glade. He thought she might not answer him, but then she said, "I'd never hear the end of it. I wouldn't have any freedom if people knew what I could do. Every dying child would be at my door. The gods require balance. I can't be toying with life and death at every whim."

He raised an eyebrow. "Then you understand why I prefer to be known for a simpler calling."

Her expression turned impassive. Was she judging him now that she knew his secret? Being a barber wasn't glamorous, but it was a needed and respectable profession. And what about her secrets?

"So you can control all animals. You sing the vermin off your customers?"

"I always hum while I work. They never ask why."

"Fascinating. And it works on all living creatures?"

"The larger the animal, the more draining it is for me, but yes. Humans are the most difficult."

"But the spell you did in the stone room, that was not from singing but sorcery?"

He snapped his fingers, and a spray of sparks lifted toward the sky.

"Ooh!"

"As impressive as it may seem, my abilities are rather limited without my voice. My song focuses my magic. Without it, I tend to make mistakes, like today when I vastly miscalculated the amount of air I would need inside my containment spell."

She pushed herself off the rock. "We should keep moving. Who knows what dangers lurk in the shadows here?"

Orpheus balked. "Wait, aren't you going to tell me?"

"Tell you what?"

"I told you about my heritage. About my powers. Aren't you going to divulge to me how you managed the healing and the mask?" He held out his open palms to her, beseeching her to be forthcoming.

"Why? It sounds like you've got me all figured out already!" She snorted sarcastically.

He rolled his head on his neck and groaned. "It is a wonder no man has snatched you up with that sweet and conformable personality."

"My personality is no better or worse than the company I keep."

He waved her off like a fly and headed for the water.

"What are you doing?"

"I'm going to enjoy a drink of this sweet water. All that singing has left my throat dry and my body weak."

The noise that came from Alena's throat could only be interpreted as an unfavorable appraisal of his intelligence.

"You don't approve of my slaking my thirst?"

"Are you an imbecile? Don't you know anything about the gods and their tests?" She dug in her bag and removed a crystal with a pale green tint.

He squatted down beside the shore. The water was as clear as any he'd ever seen and felt cold against his fingers. He cupped his hand.

"Don't drink that!" She shook her head like he was an idiot.

"Why not?"

"Everyone knows you never eat or drink anything in the realm of the gods. It's how they curse you. You drink that and you could be trapped here for all eternity, or... or—"

"Or what?"

"It is said the goddess Circe transformed a man into a pig with a cup of wine."

Alena was right. Orpheus remembered the stories from his childhood and the warnings about the gods. But as he tried to stand and turn away from the stream, the light played off the water and his mind turned as blank and empty as the silvery sky above. He lowered himself again to the stream's shore.

Cupping his palm, he scooped a handful of water and sniffed it. "It smells fresh and sweet." He was so thirsty. Soothing whispers seemed to float off the waves. *Drink. The water is pure. Drink.*

"Please! Don't!" Alena called from behind him. She held up the stone in her hand and rushed to his side, then quite suddenly backed away. "Orpheus, the water is casting a spell on you. Come toward me. Turn away from it."

He shot her a flirtatious smirk, feeling light-headed and mischievous. "I'll make you a deal, my lovely—you tell me the origins of your power, and I won't drink this water."

Alena's eyes widened and she gestured anxiously. "Come closer, away from the water, and I will tell you all you wish to know."

Orpheus again tried to move to her, but the water danced in his peripheral vision, singing to him. His throat burned as if he'd swallowed a hot stone. If he could first quench his thirst. One sip, that was all he needed. He squatted back down and dunked his fingers under the cool surface.

"No, please wait!" Alena cried, holding out her hand to him.

He ignored her and scooped a handful to his lips. Delicious, cool refreshment soothed his burning throat. It was the sweetest water he'd ever tasted. He cupped both hands together beneath the surface again and drank more, then splashed his face.

"You must try this, Alena. It's fresh. And perfectly good. Nothing is happening to me—"

His breath hitched, cutting off his thought as the world began to spin.

Men! Alena planted her hands on her hips and watched in horror as Orpheus's nose stretched toward her like pulled clay. His arms followed, extending toward the ground even as his stomach swelled and his feet morphed into grotesque clubs. The process looked painful, but the transformation occurred quickly. When it was over, Orpheus had become a bristly gray donkey with particularly long ears and a woolly face.

"Hades! By the gods, Orpheus, I told you not to drink it!" At least he'd finally moved away from the cursed water. She rushed to him and guided him safely away from its influence.

Orpheus brayed woefully at her.

"At least the gods have a sense of humor. You are officially an ass on the outside as well as in." She grabbed the donkey by the cheeks and gave the brown-eyed beast a pitying look. "I warned you. The door promised challenges. The sphinx was one. This was another. The gods are full of trickery."

He stomped his hooves.

Alena had no trouble deciphering what he was trying to express with his donkey tantrum. "Yes, I can fix you. We're lucky in that regard. I was worried you'd drop dead."

Orpheus dipped his head and nosed under her elbow.

"Oh no, I can't do it now. The water you drank needs time to... uh... leave your system. Until then, well, we ought to move on." She attempted to climb on his back, but he shied away. She spread her hands and shrugged. "It will be faster if I ride you."

The donkey smiled at her and gave her a furry wink.

"Ugh. That is not what I meant, and you know it."

He bobbed his fuzzy eyebrows and wiggled his back.

"Oh, you accept these circumstances now that you know you will be between my thighs?" She had to laugh. Only Orpheus would suffer transformation into a beast only to retain his lecherous attitude.

The donkey neighed. Face burning, she approached him again and, with some effort, climbed onto his back. Orpheus bent his neck and gave her one last annoyed look with his long donkey face.

"I told you not to drink it. You should have listened to me. I have a stone in my bag that tests for poisons and curses. I tried to use it, but you wouldn't back away from the water. I was afraid you were enthralled by... water sprites or something even more dangerous." She shrugged. "I couldn't get close enough to help you without risking my own mind. Truly, you should thank me. Had I attempted to pull you away, we might have both fallen under the spell of the water, and then where would we be?"

Orpheus gave a snort.

"We have to keep moving."

He folded his ears back, clearly disgruntled, but nevertheless saw the wisdom in her words and started down the path again. For a long time, their surroundings were quite pleasant. Rolling hills, gold and silver flowers, silver sky. At first Alena expected the sphinx or another magical creature to attack around every bend, but eventually she allowed herself to relax and enjoy the journey. Only when their progress became monotonous did she speak again.

"There's another reason I was suspicious about the water. I mean besides the books I've read about the gods."

Orpheus didn't stop walking, but his ears rotated back toward her.

"I'm a descendant of Circe."

Orpheus paused on his donkey legs and craned his neck. She saw her reflection in one large brown eye.

"Keep walking or I will not continue this story."

He started forward again.

"My father told me when I was six years old. I'd accidentally turned an earthworm into a mouse. Transformation was sort of Circe's claim to fame, and I was born with the skill as well as a talent for working with plants and herbs. My father told me that many generations before I was born, Circe's son, Telegonus, had a certain indiscretion with a mountain nymph, which resulted in my ancestor's birth. Honestly, it was so long ago. I wasn't sure I should believe it, but it accounts for my abilities."

He bobbed his head and chuffed.

"You know, I think I'm going to miss this quiet and introspective side of you. When I change you back, maybe I'll forget to recover your voice."

This time when Orpheus stopped, he did not look back at her. His long ears twitched.

"I was joking, Orpheus. You don't have to stop."

He didn't move but raised his donkey head and pointed

with his fuzzy chin. A massive wall rose in the distance, thick fog swirling at its base.

"That looks ominous." She slid off his back and gave in to the irresistible urge to scratch him behind the ears. He didn't seem to mind. "I think it's time I turned you back, don't you?" she said, cradling his nose. "Whatever is behind that wall might view an ass as their next meal. At least as a man you might stand half a chance of surviving."

She opened her satchel and began mixing herbs in her mortar, mashing them together with her pestle. Once they'd formed a thick paste, she held the mixture up to his muzzle. "Eat this."

He sniffed the concoction, sneezed, and turned his head away.

"It's not ambrosia, but certainly you can choke it down. I can't turn you back without it." She thrust it under his nose again.

He brayed and showed his teeth but eventually found his courage and managed to swallow it. His gut and throat undulated, and she worried he might spit it out. That would be unfortunate. She didn't have enough herbs with her to make another mash. Praise Zeus, he managed to eat it all.

The change happened quickly. All the hair on the donkey's back dropped off, and he stood straight up. His nose receded into his face, the bottom of his legs transformed into sandals, and before Alena could thank or curse the gods that his clothing had transformed with him, Orpheus was again standing before her, fully human. He rubbed his back with both hands and fixed her with an accusatory stare. But when he opened his mouth, only a bleat came out.

He gasped.

"I promise you, that isn't intentional. I was joking before.

Give it a moment." Alena laughed softly.

After clearing his throat, Orpheus managed to say, "It's about time!"

"I was tempted not to change you back at all." Alena stood from her spot next to the tree.

"That's not funny." He grabbed her by the shoulders, his eyes narrowing on her face. "Tell me the truth. You didn't need to wait, did you? That excuse about the water needing to move through my system was all a lie."

"What makes you think so?"

"No water has left me, woman. In fact, I rather need to void myself at this very moment."

She shrugged and pointed toward the wall. "But look how close we are to the next challenge. We could never have traveled that fast on foot."

He scoffed. "You used me!"

Crossing her arms over her chest, she rolled her eyes at him. "Gods, don't I know what that feels like."

He grunted defensively. "I did not use you that night or ever. I rather cared for you. It was you who refused me after those harpies embarrassed you, remember?"

"Because you lied to me. We kissed. We did... *things*. I told you stories I'd never told anyone." She whispered the last part as if someone might hear her, her cheeks warming as she said the words.

"I didn't lie. I simply allowed you to believe a lie. There's a difference."

She snorted.

"I admit that I knew you thought I was an archon and did not correct your misconception. I apologize for that."

She glared at him out of the corner of her eye. "How big of you."

"But you should admit that, had you known the truth

about me, you would never have spent time with me. You, Alena, are an elitist."

She scoffed in denial, but internally the accusation made her pause. It had all started with his hair—his beautiful, natural hair. That's what had caught her attention on the ship. Very few men wore their hair the way he did. Most shaved to keep vermin at bay. His hair was his own, not a wig. She'd thought he must be a man of wealth and importance to have kept his own hair. Hers was natural as well, but she had magic to thank for that. It had never occurred to her that his might be the product of magic as well. The dark waves had been and still were a delight and fascination to her.

So when three crew members had suggested his wealth came from his station as a magistrate of Athens, an archon, she'd believed it. He'd captivated her with his Greek complexion and fine garb, and they'd talked late into the night for the entire voyage.

"It was humiliating." She remembered the way the old women had looked at her when she'd admitted who she thought he was. They'd corrected her in the most public way and made her feel like a harlot for arriving to the feast on his arm. "I might have given you a chance if I'd known the truth." But even as she said it, she knew it was a lie. New to Alexandria, she'd wanted to get to know people who could help her position, not cut her hair.

"Hmm. I'm sorry you were embarrassed, and I should have told you the truth about my occupation, but nothing else was a lie. What I told you about my father was true—he did not agree with me leaving Athens. He thought my coming to Egypt was a sin. And what you told me about your mother's death—"

"I don't want to talk about it."

He placed his hand on her shoulder and, with his other, swept her into his arms.

"What are you doing?"

"I wasn't using you, Alena. And as for your comment when we were in the stone room about the other woman you saw coming out of my abode, I have not and will never be interested in her. She loiters around my shop. That is all. I haven't stopped thinking about you since the moment I met you on that fated vessel. As for the feast, I would have told you the truth if those ancient biddies hadn't poisoned you against me. I allowed the rumor that I was an archon to persist because it was a distraction, an explanation for my wealth that kept my magic a secret. If you'd only forgive me—"

"What? What would happen if I forgave you?" She searched his face. There was so much there in his expression, so much pain and longing. He was sorry; she could tell that with certainty. And his regret seemed genuine. But could she trust his intentions were pure?

Before she could take another breath, he kissed her. At first her body stiffened in resistance to the unexpected affection. She arched against his arm in a half-hearted attempt to pull away. But the longer his lips pressed against hers, the more impossible it became to fight the kiss. She tilted her head and trailed her fingers up his neck, threading them into the hair behind his ears. Parting her lips, she let him in. Into her mouth, into her heart again.

The kiss ignited a delicious heat that traveled from her lips to her toes. It warmed her and wooed her. She'd spent many long nights cursing Orpheus as a liar and scoundrel, but this kiss didn't lie. She found it impossible to maintain the walls she'd erected against him. It was too difficult. Chances were that her life would end today or tomorrow.

She didn't have the energy to waste on hating him any longer. Not when his touch made her heart beat for what seemed like the first time since the last time they'd kissed.

He made a distinctly male sound deep in his chest that rumbled against hers. She sighed into his mouth as he gently pulled away. Their eyes met, his that deep, arresting blue that always hastened her pulse. She wondered how he'd describe hers. They were also blue, although lighter than his, just like her father's. Her aunt had once said she had ghost eyes. The woman had found them eerie against her pale skin and midnight-black hair. If he thought them strange, Orpheus didn't say so. There was nothing but desire in his expression.

"I forgive you."

"All it took was a kiss?" he said softly. "I would have done that sooner had I known and if I could have gotten close enough to you." His large hands stroked along her waist, and he lowered his forehead to rest against hers.

"I suppose you needed only to offer me a ride across town on your back."

"The secret to the heart."

Her gaze dropped to the pathway. "I don't want to spend my last hours on earth hating you. And, honestly, if we ever get out of this alive, I want to kiss you like that for many hours."

"Hours...," he repeated, his lips brushing her cheek. "Indeed, I could kiss you for hours."

Lightning cracked across the sky, and they both looked up.

"A warning from the gods." He scowled.

She released him and turned back toward the wall. "There's only one way we're getting out of this alive. We have to find that grimoire and bring it to Cleopatra."

CHAPTER SIX

Orpheus tried to understand what had just happened. When he'd kissed Alena, a piece of his heart had somehow passed through his throat to his lips and into her, and now it was walking away from him, sashaying toward an ominous door in a wall that looked to be constructed out of solid stone by the gods themselves.

It made him nervous. He respected Alena and found himself disconcertingly invested in the welfare of the sorceress. He needed more time. Time to woo her. To worship her. To wed her, if that's where this was going. The wall was a reminder that their time was short. She was right though: the only way out was to face what was ahead of them. They must find the grimoire.

"Wait," he called. He caught up to her before she could try the door. "It could be dangerous."

"I'm sure it is dangerous, but the path leads here. This is where we must go." Without hesitation, she pushed against the door and groaned. "It's locked."

He shook his head, beguiled by her bravery and determination. He desperately hoped that tenacity wouldn't cross into foolishness. He took a closer look at the door, running his hands along the edges. "It's not locked. It's a false entrance. Look here. There are no hinges. This is solid stone only carved to look like a door."

"How do we get inside?"

"There are symbols here." The way the door was designed, Orpheus had to stand with his back against it to read the strange markings on his right and left. He reached out and placed his fingers on the symbols on either side of his body.

"Orpheus!"

Alena's scream cut off, and he was transported to the other side of the wall, to a strange interior room lit by burning torches. "Alena? Put your hands against—"

She arrived where he had, right in front of him. "The tricks you teach me," she said around a smile.

He shook his head and placed his hands on her shoulders. "I'd like to teach you a few more."

"How about teaching me what this place is and what we're supposed to do next?"

Orpheus scratched the back of his head and took a closer look at his surroundings. There was nothing here but a couple of torches and a dark, narrow entrance that led to the gods knew where.

"Only one possibility." He pointed toward a dark doorway.

Alena removed a torch from the wall and handed it to him. "Might as well be able to see what's going to kill us." She took a second torch for herself.

Orpheus led the way. The narrow corridor stretched on until they reached a fork. "Left or right?"

Alena stared at the symbols in the stone for a moment.

44

"Left is marked by the symbol for the underworld, right by the symbol for the god of war.

"How do you know that? These symbols are gibberish to me."

She shrugged. "I'm not sure. The symbols aren't anything I've ever seen, but I can understand them."

"Another gift from your ancestors?"

"Maybe."

"So which way do we go?" Orpheus held his torch in the entrance to the left passageway.

Nothing, although the smooth stone corridor soon became jagged with rubble. It appeared as if the walls themselves were crumbling. That might be hard to navigate.

He swung his torch around and pointed it toward the right. A skeleton dangled from the far wall, held in place by an arrow through the skull and what remained of decaying flesh. Another skeleton was propped in the corner, its lower jaw open in an eternal scream.

"Left," he said. "This may come as a surprise to you, but I'm a magician, not a warrior. Considering I don't have a weapon aside from this torch, our chances of survival seem better in the land of the dead."

She nodded, swallowing hard at the sight of the skeleton. "Agreed. I don't know the first thing about fighting. Death we may have a chance against."

She raised her torch and turned left. They picked their way through the fallen stones as the pathway turned and descended.

"What do you know about the underworld?" Orpheus asked.

"It depends. The Egyptian concept of the underworld is called Duat, and it is a place where souls are judged by Osiris and either given a peaceful afterlife or destroyed."

"I'm beginning to think we should have gone right."

"I don't think this place is ruled by Egyptian gods. So far everything we've faced has aligned more closely with the Greek gods than the Egyptian ones."

"The sphinx is Egyptian."

"In Egypt, they believe the sphinx to be benevolent. Only the Greek sphinx tells riddles and kills as the one we faced did."

He raised an eyebrow. "I never knew."

"Also, the cursed stream. That's very like Athena. She would know who my mother was and take pride in transforming me into an ass if I had fallen for it. Now we're in a labyrinth leading to the underworld. I have a feeling this is Hades's doing."

"Athena and Hades are Greek gods. Why would Greek gods be protecting a secret grimoire that was promised to Cleopatra by the Egyptian gods?"

"I have no idea. Although, Cleopatra's ancestors were originally from Macedonia. She is Greek. She thought the golden peacock represented the Eye of Horus, but what if that was a misinterpretation?"

"If it is, it explains why we, two Greek sorcerers, have been successful where Cleopatra's priests were not."

The passage narrowed, and the air grew close and hot. Orpheus had to walk sideways to fit his shoulders through and held the torch in front of him as if the fire could scare away the dark feeling that had permeated his bones.

"Before this, have you ever thought the gods were testing you?"

He glanced back at Alena, her pale blue eyes twinkling at him in the firelight. "A few times."

"Tell me."

He cleared his throat, thinking about where to begin. "When I was seven, I was tending our sheep for my father. My mother was ill, and he needed to see to her. He didn't normally leave me with the sheep, so I was nervous, afraid I wouldn't do a good job. Sure enough, one of my charges became entangled inside some brambles on the side of the mountain. If the lamb freed itself, it would likely fall to its death. If it stayed where it was, I needed to find a way to rescue it."

"What did you do?"

"I knew I was different by that point. My father used to call me blessed. He'd told me about Medea, and I knew my power was somehow linked with my voice. But I didn't know what to do. And then I had the strongest feeling that someone was watching me. Judging me. That it was a test by the gods to see if I was worthy of my power. So I sang. I sang and watched the sheep free itself and climb up the side of the mountain to me. And when it was finally in my arms, I could have sworn I saw a man fly toward the heavens, wearing winged shoes."

Alena grinned. "Hermes!"

He nodded, reached another fork in the labyrinth, and after checking with her, led her left. "When I was sixteen, my mother died." He heard her inhale sharply. "My father built a funeral pyre, and we watched her body burn. I got the same feeling, standing next to my father as her body went up in smoke. I was being watched. Watched and judged."

"What did you do?"

"I sang, and the animals did too. Crickets chirped, birds sang, dogs howled. It was sad and wonderful. It scared my father a little. It's not often you see animals sing for the dead. And when I was done, I saw a woman watching me, a glowing woman as bright as a star, with an owl on her shoulder."

"Athena?"

"I believe so." He glanced back at her again, seeking out her gaze. "The night I first kissed you, something similar happened."

For a moment their eyes locked, and then he slowly turned his attention back to the labyrinth.

Her voice broke when she spoke next. "What did you see after we, um...?"

"Nothing but a soft rustle and an abandoned golden arrow."

"Eros," she whispered.

"Maybe." He turned the corner. "There's something here. The labyrinth is opening up." He breathed a sigh of relief.

A cold blast gusted through the corridor, extinguishing their torches. Alena made a strangled sound deep in her throat.

"There's a light up ahead," he said to comfort her.

When they emerged from the passageway, his eyes adjusted to the strange ambient light of the cavernous space. The silver sky had been replaced with a red glow from the ceiling that tinged everything the color of blood. He shivered, accepting that they must move forward but terrified of what challenges the red chamber held in store. The rocky floor of the corridor gradually blended into sand under his feet, and he realized he was standing at the edge of dark water that stretched like glass beyond the edge of a crimson beach. The path they were on led directly to the shore.

"Are we supposed to swim?" Alena asked from behind him.

"I think that would be a very bad idea." Orpheus pointed across the water.

A dark figure flowed toward them, robes floating eerily in the now windless cavern, skeletal hands rowing the paddle.

"You said that symbol in the labyrinth signified the underworld... I think *this* is the river Styx."

CHAPTER SEVEN

The deathly figure Alena recognized as Charon steered his boat next to the dark shore, and she suppressed a strong desire to run and hide. She'd read about this creature who rowed travelers along the river Styx for a fee. The way the path ended at the water's edge, it was clear the only way to keep searching for the grimoire was to travel on his boat.

Bony fingers extended from the tattered sleeves of his obsidian robe and turned upward, flexing imploringly.

"He requires payment."

Orpheus's shoulders slumped. "I can't sing us out of this one. Tell me you have a couple obols in that bag of yours."

She shook her head. "No, but maybe…"

Scanning the beach, Alena's eyes landed on a circular shape protruding from the sand. Abandoning her extinguished torch on the beach, she turned her back to Charon and used her toe to dig a sand dollar from the sand. She returned to Orpheus with the disk-shaped creature cupped in her hands between them. "It's close to the size and shape of a drachma. Here goes nothing."

"Wait. You should kiss me first."

She raised her face to his. He was warm and alive, a comfort among their dark and deadly surroundings. "What? Why?"

"For luck." His eyes flashed. "And because I want you to kiss me again before I die. Do it now before you have time to think yourself out of it."

They were close, his breath mingling with hers. His dark beauty made her insides tingle. What did she have to lose? There were no whispering women here. No one to see. She couldn't resist. She rose up on her toes and pressed her lips to his.

His fingers tangled in her hair and he said into her mouth, "You can do this. I believe in you."

"*Metamórfosi*," she whispered, concentrating on the sand dollar. The animal turned cold in her hand. She looked down to find one silver drachma in her palm, more than enough to pay Charon's fare.

Orpheus ran his thumbs along her jaw. "Brilliant. I knew it. I knew the first moment I met you."

She pulled back, the muscles around her mouth tightening. What did that mean? Was he only interested in her for her power? He seemed to notice her mood shift and his eyes darkened.

"I knew the moment I met you that you were cunning and talented. Does this upset you?"

She looked away as her face grew hot.

He sighed heavily. "How long will the transformation last?"

"I'm not sure. I've never done it before."

"Then we'd better go."

She glanced between the drachma and the boat. "Yes."

At first he didn't move. Neither of them did. They stood there, staring at one another as if they were assessing a new statue in the temple. But then Orpheus grabbed her hand and led her to Charon, where she placed the coin into the skeleton's waiting palm.

The spectral figure gestured for them to climb on board. Alena cringed as she slipped through the cold aura of Charon's presence to get to the front of the boat. But once the warmth of Orpheus's body was beside her and he wrapped his steadying arm around her shoulders, she could almost forget their harrowing circumstances. She leaned into his side, trying her best to absorb his heat, and he placed a tender kiss on her temple.

"Thank you," she mumbled.

He gave her a small nod. Slowly the boat began to move.

Alena stared at the water, at the strange pale plants that wavered under the surface as Charon's boat passed. "Are those...?"

Faces stared up at her, pale, decaying corpses locked into a weedy eternity. She swallowed the scream that built in her throat.

Orpheus gripped her jaw and turned her face toward him. "Don't look," he whispered into her ear. "Look at me. I'm right here."

Thankful for the escape, she buried her face in his chest. His steady breath in her ear calmed her. Tucked into the cocoon of his embrace, she could almost forget they were careening across a river of the dead toward their probable doom.

The boat came to rest on the opposite shore, and Orpheus swept her by the waist, out of the boat and along the path away from Charon before she could blink. A screech the likes of which Alena had never heard before came from the direction of the boat—Charon.

"The drachma is a sand dollar again," she said.

The dark figure swung its scythe in their direction, slicing through the foliage behind them.

"He can't leave the boat, but I'm not sure how far he can throw that scythe. Come on. The path leads that way."

He pointed toward a house at the center of the island, and they gladly hurried away from Charon.

"What is this place?"

"I'm sure our next deadly trial. Hopefully one that will end in us finding the grimoire."

They reached the stone manor, and she allowed him to take her hand and lead her inside like a child. With a grand stone entrance and a suspiciously open door, the house welcomed them, bursting of the scent of baking bread. A fire blazed in the grate.

Alena eyed a chair near the hearth. "Can we rest? Just for a moment? I'm so tired." She rubbed her temples.

"Not here. It's too exposed."

He led her up a flight of stairs to a hall of rooms. Each, upon inspection, was empty.

"We're alone here," Orpheus said, standing in the doorway of the last room. White curtains blew in from the open window, and a plush white bed waited at the center. On the bureau rested a pitcher and a bowl of fresh fruit.

"Someone has been here. The fruit is fresh." Alena yawned.

"It could be a trap." Orpheus rubbed his face as if he too struggled to keep his eyes open.

Alena reached into her satchel for the enchanted stone she used to test for curses and poisons. Crossing to the side table, she dunked it in the pitcher of water. It did not change color.

"This water is pure. We can drink it." She poured a glass and drank it down, slaking her thirst, then dug into the bowl of fruit, holding the stone against a shiny red apple. "This is safe to eat."

Orpheus breathed a sigh of relief and closed and locked the door behind him. "We'll rest here, take shifts. Just for a little while."

He joined her at the bowl, drinking his fill and then taking a bite of the apple. Alena chose a cluster of grapes from the dish and popped one into her mouth. She poured a small amount of water into the basin and washed her face and hands. Her basket had grown heavy on her shoulder. She removed it and moaned at the relief. She rolled her neck.

"Lie down. I'll keep watch."

Resisting the draw of the white bed was futile. She crawled under the covers and laid her head on the pillow. Orpheus shifted uneasily, his eyelids heavy with sleep.

She held out her hand. "Come. Lie beside me. Just a short sleep, and then we will continue on. We're safe here." She wasn't sure how she knew they were safe, only that she felt it to her bones.

Orpheus inhaled deeply. "We can't trust the gods."

Alena could barely comprehend what he was saying. Her eyelids were heavy, and the light in the room rippled as she edged toward sleep.

Whatever strength or resolve he'd had abandoned him quickly enough. He approached her outstretched hand and slipped into bed beside her.

CHAPTER EIGHT

O rpheus told himself he'd keep watch. He didn't trust
the gods or this strange house in the underworld.
But despite his resolve, no sooner had he stretched out
beside Alena and settled her head upon his chest than he
drifted to sleep. When he woke, he felt refreshed, which was
odd, because it appeared no time had passed. The light
streaming through the sheer window dressing shone on the
floor in the very same place it had when he'd crawled
into bed.

"Oh, that felt good." Alena ran her hand down his chest
and over his stomach. She paused, seeming to catch herself,
and removed it to her side. "I'm sorry. I don't know what
came over me."

But Orpheus caught her wrist and placed her hand back
on his torso. He loved it when she touched him. Her heat.
Her scent. He brought her fingers to his lips and pressed a
kiss against the tips.

"Orpheus..." She stared at him through hooded eyes.

He reached for her and rolled her on top of him. The
look of surprise on her face made the corner of his mouth

twitch. Let her be surprised. This was what she did to him. His cock was hard as stone, and all he wanted to do was bury himself in her. He wouldn't hide it. Not anymore. Not when his every waking thought and dream was of her.

"We should—" Alena seemed to forget what she'd been about to say.

For several heartbeats he stared up at her, believing she was the most beautiful woman he'd ever laid eyes on.

"You are and always will be the one who holds my heart, Alena." He tucked her hair behind her ear. "If we ever make it out of this, I'm going to marry you properly and make the Alexandria elite regret the day they suggested you were anything less than my queen."

She laughed. "I know you're only saying that because you think we won't make it out of here, but I'd love to see the looks on their faces."

Willing his expression to be as serious as he could make it, he reached up and cupped her face. "Marry me, Alena."

Her lips twitched as if she believed he was joking at first, then fell as she examined his face. "Yes."

Her lips lowered to his, her mouth hungry, wanting. He rolled them over and settled his weight between her thighs. The woman was a rare beauty. Orpheus exulted in the feel of her soft breasts pressed into his chest. He trailed his kisses down her throat as his hand worked at her belt.

"Be my lover, Alena. We may never have another chance. I swear I will wed you if we survive, but for now…"

Alena arched beneath him, rubbing against him through the thin layers of their clothing. Gods, he wanted her. He ached to be inside her. But he wouldn't force her. No, if she wanted him to stop, he would, even if he had to handle things himself. His hand worked under her tunic and found her tight flesh.

"Alena?" He rose off her, allowing cool air to snake between their bodies. "Will you have me?"

"Yes," she said, tears glistening in her eyes. "I want this. I want to have you before we die."

Orpheus tossed her belt aside and pushed her tunic higher on her hips and then over her head. Her exposed breasts plumped, luscious and peaked, over the gentle roundness of her belly and the mound of her sex. Gods, she was a feast, and he intended to taste every part of her. He removed his loincloth and pulled off his chiton.

"I…" She covered herself with her hands as he knelt on the bed between her knees. "I've never done this before." Her tense, almost worried expression gave him pause.

"Touch me, Alena," he commanded. When she looked away, he repeated in a firm but gentle voice, "Do not be afraid. Look at me. Touch me."

She moved her hand tentatively to stroke her nails up his thigh, her eyes settling on his face. This wouldn't do. Alena was a lion, not a scared little bird. He removed her hand from his thigh and wrapped her fingers around his cock. Her eyes grew large, but he didn't stop there. He guided her touch along his length.

"This is what you like?" Her voice was husky.

"Yes. Now let's find out what you like."

He cupped her breast, weighing it in his hand before rolling her nipple between his fingers. She gasped, her eyes closing. He leaned forward to pull that nipple into his mouth and smoothed his palm down her side. When his fingers found her center, he took his time, rubbing circles until she writhed on the bed beneath him.

"Please," she begged.

He did not make her wait.

Positioning himself, he entered her slowly, allowing her

body to adjust around him. Oh, she was tight, soft, and warm. He moved above her, supporting himself on his elbows so he wouldn't crush her. She wrapped her legs around his hips as he slid in deeper.

"What is this magic?" she asked into his jaw.

"You haven't felt anything yet." He pulled out slowly, then thrust into her until she made a high-pitched moan.

"More," she cried.

He was relieved by her demand. No more could he restrain himself. He pounded into her, his hips thrusting until reality blurred and he caught himself coasting toward a bright light. She dug her nails into his back, and he was there, pitching over the edge into the abyss, her body wrapped around his as they soared above everything.

A moment later, he collapsed beside her, panting.

"That's not what I expected," she said.

"What did you expect?"

She propped herself on her elbow. "I didn't think it would feel like..." She ran her hand up her torso and wrapped her fingers around the base of her throat. "Like flying and falling all at the same time."

He gave her a lazy smile and rolled onto his back. "Well, I for one would like to send you to the stars again sometime soon."

She trailed her fingers along his sternum. "I'd like that very much."

Orpheus was nothing if not a man who loved a challenge. He reached for her once again.

CHAPTER NINE

Alena understood they should be continuing with their quest, but she couldn't bring herself to get out of bed. They'd made love more than a dozen times, and still she wanted more—more passion, more kisses, more pleasure. More unadulterated love which he poured over her with whispers like prayers in her ears as they worshipped at the altar of each other. Her heart pounded in her chest, and with every beat, she only thought of Orpheus. Beside her, he was hard in all the right places and as handsome as the first day she'd seen him. Just thinking about the way he'd moved inside her, again and again, made her flush with heat.

How long had they been in this room? Hours? The light was the same. Although, considering they were in the underworld, she wasn't sure if it ever changed.

"Would you have done this with me if we were not about to die?" he asked her, his eyebrow arching.

The question surprised her. "I wouldn't have had the opportunity. We weren't speaking to each other."

"I was speaking to you. It was you who was avoiding me."

"I thought… I thought you were only after one thing."

"And now that I've had it? What now?"

"You tell me."

"If it were up to me alone, and if we survive this quest, I'd like to have the rest of you."

"You'd have the rest of me? It seems there is none of me you haven't tasted yet." She lifted the sheet and looked down at herself, eliciting a small laugh from Orpheus.

"I wasn't kidding when I said I'd like to marry you."

"We hardly know each other." Aside from the time they'd been together on the ship, she'd spent more time hating him than in his company.

"I know you. I know you better than anyone. You are a descendant of Circe and one of the most powerful sorceresses alive. I know you heal the villagers for free when they can't pay you. I know you can read and write, which is admirable on its own, and that you also enjoy it. And I know you'd make an excellent wife. Also, I know you could have chosen to turn me back into a human immediately at the stream, but you wanted to teach me a lesson."

She flashed him a crooked smile. "Maybe."

"I forgive you." He rolled her on top of him. "Would it be so terrible to be married to a barber?"

"A barber who can charm the birds with his own voice and who kisses like Eros himself."

"How do you know how Eros kisses?"

"I don't, only that your kisses are the finest in the world."

Was her mind playing tricks on her, or had he just blushed? Her stomach growled.

"Let me get you some fruit," he said, rising from the bed. He paused, staring into the bowl.

"What is it?"

"The bowl is full."

She sprang from the bed, another pang of hunger rippling through her stomach. "The water pitcher is full again too."

They looked at each other in horror. "How long have we been in that bed, Alena?"

Her eyes searched the room for any clue, but the light hadn't changed; the temperature was exactly the same. Her gaze fell on her apothecary basket. Hand trembling, she reached down and drew a finger through a layer of dust that had settled on the top. At least a day's worth of dust, maybe more.

"Orpheus, something isn't right."

"I feel strange. Weak. Like we haven't eaten in days."

She opened her basket and retrieved a sprig of enchanted mint from one of the jars. "For clarity." She popped it into her mouth, chewed, and swallowed.

Almost instantly, the room changed. Paint peeled from the walls, the drapes hung in torn shreds in front of the window, the bed became a filthy, dusty, and stained mess, and it was hot, as hot as where they most certainly were —Hades.

"We need to leave here, Orpheus. Now."

"What do you see?"

"Get dressed."

He chose another apple from the basket. "We should take the food in your satchel."

She raised a hand to her mouth and stifled a gag. Her stomach roiled. "It is rancid. Full of maggots." She turned away and heaved, but there was nothing in her stomach to eliminate. When he still didn't put the apple down, she retrieved the rest of the mint from her bag and placed it on his tongue. As soon as the magic took effect, he tossed the rotten fruit back into the basket in disgust.

"Gods, it is another trap. But I thought you tested it!"

Alena pulled the pale green crystal from her pack and placed it in the water. It turned dark almost immediately. "It did change. I just couldn't see it through the illusion!"

Orpheus began to dress quickly. "This entire time, the gods have been slowly starving us to death."

"We should have known."

Alena tried not to reveal her shock when she saw how thin Orpheus looked. They must have been in bed for days. She finished dressing and lifted her bag onto her shoulder. But Orpheus wasn't moving.

"Hurry. We have to find the grimoire before one or both of us collapses."

"Was it *all* an illusion?" he asked her.

Their eyes met.

"No," she said quickly, surprised at how much she wanted him to know the truth about her feelings. She paused and offered him a soft smile. "Now let us live to prove it."

He nodded and charged toward the door. Her legs felt frail as she followed him into the corridor, but she pressed on. As they passed through the hall, she saw the house for what it was. Each of the rooms was filthy, some with pairs of skeletons still embracing in the beds. This was a place of forgetting. A place where one could sleep their life away.

They left the house and continued along the path they'd been following, which led up a steep hill. The climb was difficult in their debilitated state, but as they reached the top, they saw a Greek temple in the distance, its white marble pillars gleaming against the rich green of the surrounding hillside. Panting and exhausted, they helped each other across the glade and up its marble steps. There, on the altar, lay their prize, a massive golden book engraved with the same ornate peacock they'd observed on the doors.

Alena swayed on her feet and caught herself on Orpheus's arm. "Do you feel that?"

He nodded. "Power. Pure, unadulterated power."

The grimoire was as long as the full length of her arm with a width as wide as her shoulders and a thickness at least a cubit deep. It looked to Alena to be both ancient and brand-new. "How will we even carry it? It's monstrous."

She approached it cautiously, scanning the altar for any source of danger. It couldn't be as easy as just taking it. Despite the fear and foreboding flooding her senses, she forced her aching legs to move her toward the grimoire.

"Alena, look!" Orpheus pointed to her right.

The gold doors they'd come through had sprouted from the earth beside them.

"This is it then," she said, reaching for the book. "The end of the path. Let's take it and return home."

"No!" Orpheus yelled as energy crackled in her ears. He lunged for her. "Don't touch it!"

CHAPTER TEN

Orpheus stopped Alena just in time, hands gripping her wrist from behind her, his heart hammering against her back. "When you reached for it, lightning formed in the air around you like a cloud." He shook his head and wrapped his arms around her shoulders. "It's protected with strong magic."

"Of course it is." Alena's voice cracked through dry, parched lips. "Cleopatra wants vengeance. She wouldn't want this grimoire if it weren't ultimately powerful. The gods aren't going to just let us take it."

"No."

"But Orpheus, we have to try." She rotated in his arms to face him. "Look at us. We can hardly stand. If we don't seize the grimoire now and go through those doors, we are as good as dead."

Orpheus scowled. If anyone was going to touch the thing, it had to be him. He refused to put her in any more danger. He was sure now that he loved her. If they survived this test, he *would* marry her, even if he had to carry the pigheaded woman home over his shoulder. And if this grimoire was cursed, he would do his best to save Alena from it. If one of them had to risk death, it was going to be him.

Rubbing a hand across his mouth, Orpheus tried to think through his growing hunger and weakness. He licked his cracking lips. "If we knew the nature of the magic protecting it, we could use either logic or magic to defeat it."

"Yes." Alena rubbed her temples. "But in order to learn the nature of the ward, one of us would have to trigger it." She squatted to retrieve a rock from the ground near her feet and hurled it at the book, but the stone skimmed harmlessly across the cover.

"At least now we know the wards are sophisticated enough to identify an actual threat."

"What now?" Alena asked, looking up at him with terrified eyes.

Gods, she was beautiful. He stroked her hair back from her face and kissed her firmly on the lips. "Here's what will happen. I'm going to try to take the grimoire. After you see what happens to me, you will know the nature of the ward and will find a way through it."

"No! You can't. It could kill you."

"You're a healer, Alena. Whatever happens to me, you can fix. Bring me back like you did the goat."

"Please. Please don't make me. I wouldn't be able to bear it. What if I don't have the right herbs?"

He gave her a solemn smile. "Then you will go on. You'll find a way to go back, and you will live a happy life without me."

"No. No. You can't do this, Orpheus." She tugged at his arm, pleading with him.

"Why not?" Beautiful, tender Alena never failed to do

the right thing. He'd wronged her once. Didn't she understand that this time he must put her first?

"Because... because I love you, you fool." Oh, how those words fell bittersweet on his ears.

"And because I love you, I can't bear to see you in this place a moment more. I'm going to get that book. You take the grimoire back to Cleopatra." Before she could protest further, he pushed her aside and leaped toward the altar, reaching for the grimoire.

Lightning formed in a circle around him, the air so charged with power that all the hair on his body stood on end. But he never reached the book. He hung, frozen in the air, the sharp tip of a glowing blade pointed at his heart. A blinding light shaped in the silhouette of a woman appeared between him and the book.

"Gods!" Orpheus cursed and found he was able to move to shield his eyes from the light. His feet came to rest on the slab of stone in front of the altar.

"Just one," boomed a powerful female voice. "Stop, hero, and heed me."

Alena appeared beside him and took his hand in hers. Gradually the light dimmed. Standing before them was a woman as vibrant as the Euphrates, with two horns rising on either side of her dark head, framing a red solar disk. Her arms were raised, as were two colorful wings that seemed to put off their own light.

"Isis," Alena whispered, voice trembling. She bowed her head and dropped to her knees.

Orpheus thought he'd better show his respect as well and knelt beside her despite the pain it caused his aching legs. He didn't think it was a good idea to anger a goddess, especially not in the heart of the underworld.

"Rise, Orpheus, Alena. Your selfless love for each other

has proven your worth. You have overcome every obstacle the gods have put in your path. You have truly earned this grimoire. Now I must beg you to forgo your prize and leave it in this place where the gods protect it."

Orpheus felt his shoulders hunch and couldn't stop himself from speaking out. "Goddess, the gods offered Cleopatra the door. She forced us through it. We cannot go back without the grimoire or she will kill us."

Alena squeezed his hand, her expression filled with fear for him.

"Cleopatra." Isis scoffed. "She claims to be a reincarnation of me but is nothing more than a scared narcissist. It is Apopis, the Egyptian god of chaos, who whispers in her ear. Her time as ruler of Egypt is over. If she gets this book, all balance and order of things to come will be thrown into chaos and Apopis will grow in strength. He knows this and therefore revealed the door to Hades to her, knowing she'd leap at the promise of power. Thankfully, up until now the Greek gods have protected this grimoire. Its origins are from Zeus and Hera, you see. You have passed their tests and earned this grimoire, but if you allow Cleopatra to have it, she will stop at nothing until she rules the world."

Alena sat back on her heels. "As Orpheus said, if we leave without it, she will kill us."

Isis's eyes landed on their coupled hands. "The god of chaos started this, but I am the goddess of life and magic. Do not underestimate me. I will show you the way."

ORPHEUS LED ALENA THROUGH THE GOLDEN DOORS AND INTO the room where they had begun their quest. A contingent of soldiers waited for them. He hugged the golden book to his chest with one arm and held Alena in the other. He didn't plan to let her out of his sight.

When the guards reached for the grimoire, he pulled away. "I can only give the book to Cleopatra herself. No one else!"

The soldiers seized him by the elbow and dragged them to the throne room. Cleopatra's kohl-lined eyes widened when she saw them. Orpheus watched her fingers bend like claws and all the tiny muscles around her mouth tighten. Beside him, Alena trembled, whether from weakness or fear, he did not know.

"So you've survived after all, despite the predictions of my advisors." She flashed the men by her side a murderous look before her gaze settled on Orpheus and then Alena. "Is that the grimoire?"

"Yes." Orpheus held out the book to her.

A soldier approached him, intending, no doubt, to carry the book to his pharaoh, but Cleopatra stopped him with a hiss.

"Only I shall touch it," she snapped. Haughtily, she descended from the dais and approached Orpheus, grasping greedily for the grimoire. Once it was in her hands, her breath quickened and she caressed it like the face of a lover.

Orpheus was relieved to be rid of the weighty tome. Gods, he was exhausted. His mouth was as dry as a stone. "Please, the quest was difficult. Allow us to leave and seek respite."

Beside him, he heard Alena's breath rush from her lungs in a shaky exhale.

But Cleopatra did not even look in his direction. She returned to her throne, rested the grimoire in her lap, and reached for the corner of the golden cover, her expression that of a child tearing into a gift. But when she opened the book, the pages were blank.

Orpheus and Alena crept backward.

"Seize them!" she yelled.

The guards grabbed them both again and forced them to their knees. Orpheus allowed his head to roll forward on his shoulders. When Isis had presented them with the decoy book, he'd been skeptical it would work. Now they were paying the price for the folly of the gods.

"What have you done?" Cleopatra seethed. She set the book aside and rushed Orpheus, grabbing his face and squeezing until her nails bit into his flesh.

"He's done nothing!" Alena blurted. "Let us go. You asked for the grimoire, and we brought it to you. That *is* what was on the other side of the door."

"It is blank. You have tampered with it." Cleopatra forced the words through her teeth.

"This is what was given to us by the goddess Isis herself," Alena yelled.

"Perhaps you must use magic to read it?" Orpheus said. His voice cracked from thirst.

"Yes. Orpheus is right. The pages are likely enchanted," Alena added. "Now please. We've accomplished your quest. Let us go! We've had nothing to eat or drink in days."

Cleopatra released Orpheus's face and returned to the book. She lifted it again and stared at the blank page inside, closing and opening the cover. She held it out to a priest who stood beside her throne. He removed the falcon's head from his scepter, lit the internal wick, sucked the flame into his mouth, and blew smoke across the page. Symbols appeared on the blank papyrus, almost as if they were alive beneath the surface.

"It's working," she said. "Again!"

"Please, my queen!" Orpheus begged.

"Go then. I tire of your presence." She dismissed them with a wave of her hand.

The guards released them, and Orpheus pivoted, placing a hand on Alena's back to guide her past the guards and toward the front of the palace. They'd taken a few long strides when screams broke out behind them. Orpheus risked a glance back to see snakes swarming from the book. One coiled and struck Cleopatra above the breast. Her eyes locked on him.

"Stop them!" Cleopatra ordered. "Kill them. Kill them now!"

Orpheus broke into a weak run as the guards closed in. They were doomed.

Alena tugged his hand. "Sing, Orpheus. Sing!"

CHAPTER ELEVEN

A lena flinched at the intensity of the sound when Orpheus heeded her request and sang. His voice rang like a bell used to call out the spirits of the dead. The melody made her want to cry, but the tone bolstered her. This song was a weapon, and he was wielding it like a sword.

The guards froze in place and the snakes poured from the book, seeming to dance to his music. They coiled and snapped. Swords clattered to the floor. Soldiers collapsed.

Alena had never seen this variety of viper, but they must be poisonous. Black veins had already extended from the place of Cleopatra's bite, and she clutched her throne as if she was in pain.

Orpheus's voice gave out, cracking from weakness and thirst. He took Alena by the arm and dragged her toward the exit. Where he got the strength, she had no idea. She was so tired she could hardly stand upright. Howls of pain behind her told her the snakes had done their duty.

"Come. Quickly," Orpheus said, ushering her around a corner and into a dark corridor.

More guards were running toward them, called forward by the screams.

"This way."

A golden glow shone from a hidden doorway. Alena slipped into a secret passageway where Isis herself greeted them. The goddess glided through the walls of the palace, the stone arranging itself at her will. A few moments later, they emerged through a narrow doorway onto the streets of Alexandria.

Night had fallen, and Alena welcomed the cover of darkness as they slipped into the city. Already they heard a commotion and screams coming from the palace. Cleopatra was dead. The country would soon be in turmoil.

"My home is this way," Alena said, pointing toward the river.

But the goddess shook her head. "Every soldier and citizen of Egypt will come looking for you. The guards will blame you for her death. It is easier to do than to tell the truth. If you stay here, they will kill you."

Alena darted a worried glance toward Orpheus, but he'd gone still as midnight water. Tears welled in her eyes. "Truly, I can go no farther."

"How do I keep her safe?" Orpheus murmured, wrapping his arm weakly around her.

When his gaze settled on her, there was no mistaking the intention behind the question. Her heart wrenched at the realization that he'd sacrifice himself for her again and again if he had to. They'd shared a deep connection in Hades. Was it possible it was all genuine and would continue now that they were back in the real world?

Isis removed a stone, shiny and veined with gold, from the folds of her dress. She held it out to them. A symbol of a tree was carved into the surface. Alena moved closer, curious about what it was.

"When the goddess Hera married Zeus, Gaea gifted her with the Garden of the Hesperides. Once you are inside this garden, your safety is assured. The creatures who live there, the garden nymphs, will see to your every need."

Alena swallowed, her heart pounding in her chest. She was tired, so tired. "Once we're inside. *If* we can get past the dragon."

"Dragon?" Orpheus asked.

"Yes, a dragon guards the entrance," Alena said. "Hera isn't keen on having uninvited guests."

"Hera," Isis said, "is too busy chasing after Zeus to know what's happening in her garden. She will never know you are there. And as for the dragon..." Her eyes focused on Orpheus.

He shook his head. "I can't sing. I have nothing left."

Alena believed him. He'd paled, and his knees were shaking. Escaping the palace had drained him.

"Orpheus, you have been called a cheater, a bastard, a louse charmer. Don't you think dragon charmer is more fitting? After all, your ancestor Medea once sang a dragon to sleep to help her lover. Won't you do the same for yours?"

"Oh, we're not—" Alena stopped short when Orpheus gave her an injured look. "We're not ready. He's too tired."

"I'm afraid we're out of time," Isis said. "If we are to have any hope of saving the lives that grow inside you, we must leave now."

"Lives?" Alena shook her head.

Orpheus was staring at her, lips parted.

"I am the goddess of life," Isis said. "And I see three burning candles within you. Three bright lights."

Alena could not believe what she was hearing. She

placed her hands on her abdomen, then looked to Orpheus for an explanation.

He turned to Isis. "I am strong enough for this. How do we get there?"

"Simply touch the stone and it will take you home." Isis extended her hand to them.

Orpheus reached for Alena, and she slid her fingers into his. She must be dreaming. All this would fade with the sunrise. People didn't talk to goddesses or travel by stone. But when she laid her fingers on the tree, the darkness seemed to wrap tighter around her, like a black blanket that squeezed out the light. When it unwrapped again, Isis was gone and they stood in the middle of an empty field.

And stared into the golden eyes of what appeared to be a very moody black dragon.

CHAPTER TWELVE

Orpheus gazed into the face of the golden-eyed dragon, his knees trembling from either weakness or fear. The beast's hide was black and as impervious to damage as a crocodile's, with scales beginning behind its horned temples and running the length of its bony body. Each of its razor-sharp teeth was as long as Orpheus was tall and could no doubt shred him in an instant. That seemed to be the dragon's general plan as it reared and glared at its prey. A golden heart shone inside its chest as if the gods had lit him internally like a lantern.

For a moment Orpheus was frozen in fear, hypnotized by the rising of its head and clacking of its claws. Would the fire in its heart spray out of its mouth and fry him to a crisp? The nostrils flared as the beast assessed him, its intelligent eyes narrowing. If nothing else, it was majestic. A majestic, beautiful beast that would soon eat him.

"Orpheus, sing!" Alena commanded desperately.

He glanced back at her. Three lights. Isis had seen three lights. He couldn't die today. He had a family to protect and a woman he must make his wife. And if the goddess could be believed, three future children to raise. He'd do better than his father. He swore he would.

"Orpheus!" Alena screamed again.

The dragon's lungs glowed behind its scales, filling with fire. The mouth opened.

Orpheus began to sing. The melody the magic gave to him was ancient, and he could imagine his ancestor Medea singing the same song, the life of her lover Jason on her mind just as Alena filled his thoughts now. With every last bit of strength he had, he poured himself into that song, beseeching the dragon to back away, to lie down, to fall asleep.

It was difficult work. Orpheus broke out in a drenching sweat, his knees turning to water under him. But he did not stop. He sang until his chest ached.

The dragon's teeth clanked shut. The fire in its chest cooled. Orpheus watched in wonder as the terrifying beast circled like a dog, then lay down, curling in on itself, its great eyes drooping and then closing fully. Orpheus reached behind him and took Alena's hand. His voice soared as he led her around the creature.

Golden gates appeared in what had been an empty field. Beyond the gates rose a breathtakingly beautiful display of flowers and trees: the Garden of the Hesperides. He pushed against the gates and found them locked. Still singing, he looked back at Alena.

She searched the ground, gouging the earth with the toe of her sandal, then digging like an animal with her fingers. Her plan became clear when she lifted a worm from the soil. "It worked with the sand dollar."

Orpheus swayed with fatigue. There would be no kiss for luck this time. He could not stop singing or the dragon might wake. He heard her whisper the incantation and then saw her turn a skeleton key in the lock of the gate. A jiggle, a crank, and a push and they were inside.

As soon as the gate was closed behind them, the key became a worm again, and Alena dropped it onto the soft earth. Orpheus stopped singing. His knees gave out, and he fell face-first into a patch of marigolds.

"Orpheus!" Alena rolled him over and shook his shoulders.

It had been days, maybe longer, since they last ate or drank anything other than cursed water or rotting fruit. He needed to... He needed to...

"We made it," he mumbled, glancing at Alena, whose beautiful face was suddenly twisted with worry. "I told you all we had to do was survive."

EPILOGUE

Survive they did. Garden nymphs, it seemed, loved to have something to tend to. Tending a garden was their true delight, and two ailing humans—that was a project they could not resist. Alena pondered that as the glittering faces of Nala and Ensing came into view, one nymph mopping Alena's brow, the other helping her balance.

"Is this normal?" Orpheus asked. "Are the babies coming?"

The nymphs nodded furiously. She hoped they were right. The pain was almost unbearable. She'd delivered babies before as a healer, but it was different when they were your own. Different when there were three. Fear wasn't an option, however. Her family needed her, and losing herself to dark thoughts wouldn't help anything.

She focused on Orpheus, the way his cheeks had rounded these past seasons on the diet of roots and berries the nymphs helped them prepare, and she wondered at his tawny arms. So strong. So true. His body had transformed into nothing but long, lean muscle since they'd been here. She thought he looked like he belonged in a garden like this, a garden of the gods. He certainly looked like a god now with his keen blue eyes and full beard. He held her up from behind as she squatted in the way the nymphs had shown her.

He'd built a cabin for her here with those arms, a small luxury to keep out the daily showers and the chill night air. And the nymphs had woven them clothing from spider-webs, soft bark, and the wool from a herd of golden sheep that called the garden home. They'd been tempted to make those sheep dinner on more than one occasion, but both they and the golden apples were strictly forbidden. The nymphs had warned them early on. The last thing they wanted to do was alert Hera to their presence.

Another birthing pain crushed her, and Alena screamed. This time her body knew what to do. With a series of contractions that seemed to bleed into the earth, one, then two, then three tiny beings were born.

"Girls," Orpheus said breathlessly. He tipped her back on a soft bed of moss and cradled her head. "Three sisters, Alena. They're perfect."

Thank the gods the nymphs knew what to do. They tended to the babies and to her as Orpheus mopped her brow and helped her bring the firstborn to her breast.

"We should call her Circe," Orpheus said, "in honor of the goddess whose magic you carry in your blood."

Alena nodded. "And this one will be Medea," she said, taking the second child from Nala's arms. The two girls had a shock of black hair and stunning lapis eyes like their father's. The third child was handed to Orpheus to allow the first two time to nurse. She might have wailed, but instead she stared at her father with wide, knowing eyes of the darkest blue. So dark, in fact, that Alena could hardly make out the black pupil at the center.

"This one is cunning and fearless," Orpheus said. "What shall we name her?"

Alena thought for a moment. "Isis. After the one who brought us here."

Ensing whispered something into Orpheus's ear, the nymph's pearlescent pink lips bending softly.

"She thinks we should name one Hera in thanks for the protection of her garden."

Alena frowned. "Hera doesn't know we're here, and I doubt she would offer her protection if she did."

Ensing lowered her gaze and looked away.

"Isis, Medea, and Circe then," Orpheus said. "Three sisters, descendants of the sorceress Medea and the goddess Circe, conceived in Hades and born in the garden of the gods. Surely they will be blessed beyond measure."

❧

MANY SEASONS LATER...

"DON'T TELL MOTHER," MEDEA SAID TO HER SISTERS, CIRCE and Isis. "I'm going to conjure something."

"Conjure something? You know Mother and Father do not like us to do complex magic without their supervision." Circe placed her hands on her hips and shook her head. "It is ill-advised. Remember that time you attempted to conjure water from the stream?"

"Water sprang from the floorboards for days," Isis said. "I swore I never wanted to see another puddle."

Medea scowled. How could her sisters hold that against her? She'd made the mistake before she was even fully grown. This was different. She was an adult now. All three sisters were women who had honed their individual talents through the years. She knew in her heart she could do this.

"Of course I remember," she said. "But it was a long time ago. I realize my mistake now. I was missing a way to focus my power." She rubbed her palms together in small circles. "Father uses his voice. I've never been any good at singing, but I knew there had to be something I could use in the same way."

Isis shifted and the shadows followed, her black eyes reflecting Medea's excitement. "Sister, are you saying you found such a way?"

Medea drew a tapered stick from the folds of her robes. "With this."

Circe gasped. "Where did you get that? I can feel it. It pulses as if it is still alive."

"I cut it from the tanglewood tree."

Both Circe and Isis took a step back at that. The tanglewood tree had sprouted the day they were born from the exact spot where their mother had birthed them. The sapling had grown strong as the three of them had, the trunk splitting into three distinct sections that twisted and tangled toward the sun. The three sisters had grown up playing in its branches, and it didn't take them long to notice that their powers grew stronger when they were near it.

Several years ago, as an act of solidarity, each of them had chosen a section and carved their names into the bark. Medea remembered well how hers had seemed to whisper to her, how her name had glowed in the bark as if the tree was lit from within. After that, it was clear each was bound to the tree just as they were bound to each other.

"From which section did you take it?" Isis asked through a tight smile.

"My own, of course," Medea promised, hand to her

heart. Under her palm, it pounded with excitement to share her new discovery with her sisters. "Don't you see? With this, the tanglewood tree is always close to me. With this... wand... I can wield my magic more effectively."

"You think you can," Circe said. "Or it might explode in your face."

Her sisters crowded around her, staring at the wand, and Medea displayed it openly for their perusal. To think what they could do if Isis and Circe made their own. How powerful they would be!

"If you die, sister, I can bring you back," Isis said darkly.

"Can you? For certain?" Fighting back a chill, Medea gave her a sideways glance.

Isis shrugged. "I've done it with animals. A baby bird that fell from a nest, a sheep born too early."

Beside her, Circe shivered. "You scare me sometimes."

Isis grinned in a way that showed all her teeth, sending goose bumps up Medea's arms. Medea swore that sometimes her sister enjoyed scaring her and Circe with her dark magic.

"So," Medea asked through an impish grin, breathless with anticipation. "Will you help me conjure something?"

"That depends. What do you plan to bring forth?" Circe asked.

Medea took a deep breath and let it out slowly. "Do you remember when Mother was teaching us our lessons and I asked her where she had learned it all from?"

"She said she learned it in a book," Isis said. "I've never seen a book."

"Neither have I," Circe said.

"It's a source of knowledge. Something that can teach us spells. If we had a book, we could grow stronger and even better at magic." The wand tingled in Medea's grip, begging her to use it.

"Oh, a book would be very exciting!" Isis rubbed her hands together.

"So will you help me?"

"Mother and Father would not approve of this." Circe chewed her lip.

Medea nudged her side and bounced on her toes. "If we do it quickly, they needn't know. They left on their walk of the gardens not so long ago. It will be some time before they return."

"But to conjure something, you must hold the thought of it in your mind in a clear and focused manner. How can you conjure a book when you have never seen a book?"

Isis placed her hand on Medea's. "We have seen one. The paper on which Mother writes her recipes. The one that she says she brought here in her basket. Not quite a book, but you can picture a stack of those papers. A stack of knowledge. A stack of *magical* knowledge."

Medea swallowed. "I think I see it in here." She pointed to her head. "I will concentrate on bringing us the most powerful book of magic that exists anywhere."

"Oh!" Circe squirmed. Of the three of them, disobeying their parents was the hardest for Circe, but even she could not deny that a book would be a welcome distraction. The garden was so boring, and it seemed they'd exhausted their parents' knowledge of magic. "Yes. Do it. Do it quickly before Mother and Father return."

Medea closed her eyes and raised the wand, allowing the power of the tanglewood tree to flow through her. She could feel the energy of the garden below the floor under her bare feet and the pulse of power she was born with deep in the marrow of her bones. With a quiet mind, she concentrated on what she thought a book must look like and her desire for the knowledge it must contain. Her entire body tensed for it. She could almost see it, glinting at the corner of her consciousness.

It was all too much. Sweat dripped down her temple, and her knees began to shake. She swayed on her feet. Isis and Circe held her up, imbuing her with their strength. Isis's strange power over life and death whirled in her veins like icy water while Circe's magic grew down her arm like a twisting vine and left the taste of basil in her mouth. Together, they ignited something fierce inside her. What was a glint at the edge of her consciousness became a rush of gold heat.

A heavy weight plowed into her chest, knocking her backward onto her bottom. The fall broke her sisters' contact with her, and their power cut off abruptly. The absence of her sisters' touch left her hollow inside. Her eyelids fluttered.

There was something in her arms. Something cold and heavy. Something gold.

"By the gods," Circe said from above her. "Are you injured?"

She shook her head but truly could hardly breathe beneath the thing. "Heavy," she rasped.

Isis and Circe reached down and together lifted the weight off her and slammed it onto the table where it rattled the wood. Medea climbed to her feet. She was holding her wand so tightly her knuckles had turned white. Shakily, she placed it back inside her sleeve.

"Is that...?" Medea took a step toward it. A massive pile of papers was clinched inside a solid gold cover. It was larger than she'd expected, larger than her entire torso.

"A book," Isis said, eyes widening.

"It worked!" Circe hugged Medea's aching shoulders.

A man's laugh cut through the window of the small cottage, and Medea stiffened. "Mother and Father are back! Come, help me hide it."

She gestured toward their sleeping chamber. Using all their strength, the three lugged the book into the room and slid it beneath her bed, covering it in their old blankets. They'd only just hidden it and returned to the hearth when their father entered the cottage.

"What have you three been up to?" His blue eyes flashed beneath a quizzical brow. Could he smell the magic in the air? He ran a tanned hand through his graying hair, seeming to war with himself over what to say next.

Medea met his gaze and shrugged, saved from having to explain by their mother's arrival.

"I'm going to harvest some herbs," Circe blurted, heading for the door at unnatural speed.

Isis's gaze darted toward Medea before mumbling, "Help me fetch water for supper?"

"Yes, sister." Medea rose and grabbed a water jug from the wall. They ignored their father's confused expression and jovially kissed their mother's cheek as they passed her outside the doorway.

They didn't stop walking or say a single word until they'd reached the tanglewood tree, well out of sight of home and their parents' prying eyes.

Medea leaned against the tree, exhaustion sending her sliding down the trunk onto her bottom. "I can hardly keep my eyes open."

"But you did it," Isis said. "Do you know what this means?"

Circe hopped up and down, her eyes twinkling with

possibilities. "It means we have a book. Oh, I wonder what secrets are inside."

"That one and more," Isis said. "Today we proved we can make things happen. Together we can bring the universe here, to us. Learn about everything from the safety of the garden."

"Or go to the world," Medea whispered.

As one, they cast a glance in the direction of the gate. Circe, rule follower that she was, shook her head almost immediately. They were not allowed outside the garden. Not ever. But Isis gave her an understanding nod. She, like Medea, was not ready to dismiss the possibility so quickly.

"What happens now?" Circe asked.

Medea held out her hand, and her sisters both clasped it. "We do as we've always done. We three sisters stay together and we make magic."

PART II
HER DRAGON GUARDIAN

CHAPTER ONE

Many seasons later...

The Garden of the Hesperides offered a paradise of fragrant blossoms, lush green trees, and delectable vegetation, roots, and berries. For Medea's entire life, this protected, sacred space, a gift from Gaea to Hera on her wedding day, had provided her and her two sisters with everything they needed to grow and thrive.

Everything until now.

Lately the garden was short of one very important thing —privacy.

Since the day their parents, Orpheus and Alena, with the help of the goddess Isis, had snuck in through the front gate, the two had lived in a simple cottage built by their father's own hands. When Alena gave birth to the three of them, Orpheus had added on a second room, and for most of their lives, that had been perfectly adequate. Until Medea, acting contrary to their parents' wishes, had conjured the golden grimoire.

She and her sisters, Isis and Circe, had spent years

studying the book in secret, as well as other books they'd covertly summoned during stolen moments alone.

Only, their thirst for knowledge had far exceeded what they could attain in tiny sips of guarded study. They needed a way to easily hide and transport the book so that they could practice the spells on its pages anywhere in the garden, not only in the confines of their chambers. The book itself had inspired their plan. A spell inside held the promise of freedom and opportunity. If this worked, it would change everything.

"Why didn't any of us think to use a spell to make this blasted thing lighter?" Medea grunted from the effort of carrying the massive tome. The thing weighed a ton. Even with her sisters gripping the corners of the sling they'd created to tote the tome from their family's cottage, the dead weight made her stagger, and fresh beads of sweat broke out across her skin.

Medea was relieved when they arrived at their intended destination, the field of ever-blooming marigolds that decorated the area near the front gate of the garden. The golden scrollwork of the front gates rose into the clouds.

She gazed through the bars into the empty field beyond and wondered at the stories she'd heard about the Guardian at the Gate. Her father had spoken of a fierce dragon with razor-sharp teeth, massive horns, and impenetrable black scales. Nothing but a small stone cottage stood on the other side of the bars. The heaviness of disappointment weighed on her heart. As afraid as she should be, her curious mind was desperate to see the beast for herself

"Medea, are you sure about this? Mother and Father would be furious if they knew we were here. It's forbidden!"

Medea whirled to find Circe's face distorted with worry as she dropped her corner of the sling and let the golden grimoire dent the field of marigolds. Circe hated to break the rules. Since they'd obtained the contraband spell book, she'd been wracked with guilt over their secret activities. Admittedly, Medea and Isis had pressured her into going along with this idea. But what was the use of having powerful magic if you couldn't use it to hide that very magic?

"They won't find out, sister," Medea said. "And if you stick to the plan and help me execute this spell, they'll never know. We can do this. We're ready."

"We're grown women and powerful witches. Why do we need to follow the rules anymore anyway?" Isis added. As always, she did not share Circe's qualms about breaking their parents' rules. Despite resembling her sisters in the most basic sense—black hair; straight nose; a pink, bow-shaped mouth—Isis had always carried an aura of darkness about her, from the deeper olive tone of her complexion to her navy-blue irises, only a fraction of a shade lighter than her pupils. Her gaze held an intensity the others did not share.

"You know why we have rules, Isis," Circe said defensively. "It's for our safety. Hera doesn't know we're here. If we break the rules, she could find out and… execute us, I suppose."

That was the story their parents had always told them anyway, although the longer Medea lived, the more she questioned if the stories were actually true or inventions of exhausted parents who needed their three rambunctious daughters to obey.

The nymphs who tended the garden had agreed to keep their secret as long as, their parents explained, they followed three simple rules. One, they must never eat the golden apples that grew in the orchard. Two, the sheep with the golden fleece that grazed along the hillside were off-limits to eat, although using their wool for weaving was permitted. And three, the rule that applied to them on this day, they weren't allowed near the garden gate.

The first rule made sense to Medea. Nothing living in the garden ever ate the golden apples. Not rabbits or the aforementioned sheep or the tiny, spindle-legged deer that frequented the brook near their cottage. The only beings that ever touched the apples were the garden nymphs who collected the ones that fell from the branches in giant baskets. None of them had any idea what the nymphs did with the apples, but they'd never seen them eat the fruit. Perhaps, Medea assumed, the fruit wasn't edible at all.

The second rule was trickier to understand. Something *did* eat the sheep. Occasionally one would go missing overnight, silently disappearing from the flock with no explanation. But Medea had a horrific memory of a loss that was not so silent. She'd awakened in the middle of the night to the bleats of panicked sheep and the distant thunder of stampeding animals. There had been blood the next morning, splattered across the hillside.

For many nights after that, she'd feared the unknown. What was killing the sheep? As far as she was aware, there were no predators in the Garden of the Hesperides. Time and again, she'd asked their father Orpheus for an explanation. He'd answered only that there were rules for a reason and if she followed them and was within the wards that protected their cottage before nightfall, she had nothing to fear. Someday, he said, when she was older, she'd understand. Now she was older and she no longer feared the mysterious sheep thief, but she still had no explanation for it.

The third rule was the most perplexing. Why couldn't

they come here to the field near the gate? She understood why they should not leave the garden of course. Their parents had explained to them that they had made enemies among the gods. Was it simply protection from being seen through the gate that their parents were after? Then again, after all this time, was anyone still watching?

"Let's get this over with," Circe muttered with an exaggerated shudder. "I don't like it here."

Isis laughed. "What is it, exactly, you hate about this place, sister? Is it the sunshine, the sea of beautiful flowers, or the idea of practicing unsupervised magic with your sisters that bothers you?"

"Knock it off, Isis. You know she hates breaking the rules." Medea had long ago accepted Circe's resistance to rule-breaking as a trait tied to her fiercely loyal heart. She ignored Isis's derisive glare and drew her wand from her sleeve, opening the book to the spell they'd agreed on.

Abruptly, Isis's head turned sharply to the side and her nostrils flared.

"What is it, sister?" Medea asked. A chill crawled along her neck at the look on her face. Unlike Circe, nothing usually rattled Isis.

"I smell smoke," she said. "And something else. Something... animal. But it's strange. Musky. It reminds me of death."

"Death?" Medea's voice cracked, and she swallowed her sudden trepidation.

Isis nodded once.

Each of them had their strengths when it came to magic.

Medea was gifted with charms and enchantments. She could levitate almost anything, train insects to sing her a song, and coax a flower to grow at twice its natural speed with a wave of her wand.

Circe was a master of transformation. She could turn a blade of grass into a snail or a fish into a frog with little effort. When it came to potions, she intuitively knew which herbs to combine to produce a tonic imbued with the desired attributes.

But Isis's talent was truly chilling. She was a master of necromancy who had raised more than one animal from the dead. Isis *knew* death. When Isis said she smelled death, Medea understood she wasn't exaggerating.

Medea shook off the sudden chill that rattled her bones. "We won't linger. Let's do this and do it quickly."

"I agree with that plan!" Circe drew her wand from the pocket in her sleeve. The six-inch length of wood was polished smooth and twisted naturally from its base to a slightly upturned tip.

Medea's wand, cut from a different section of the tanglewood tree, was a crooked seven inches that still held a hint of bark.

Isis sniffed and drew her own wand from her boot. Sleek and dark, it was only slightly longer than Circe's with an elongated knot in the wood of one side.

Since the day she'd acquired the grimoire, Medea had proved the strongest at interpreting the ancient symbols the spells were written in. To be sure, all three were gifted with the ability to read multiple languages, but the symbols in the grimoire were exceptionally ancient and interpreting them was tricky. It wasn't a language their parents had taught them. Although any of them could read the spells, truly comprehending the intention behind the words was difficult. The three sisters had experimented with each of them leading the rituals only to determine that without a doubt the outcome was better when Medea read the incantation from the page.

So, as had become their habit, Medea uttered the spell, her voice growing stronger as all three raised their wands and circled the tome. Tiny sparks of light lifted from the book and swirled between them. A growing wind blew from the pages. Power, thick and hot, teased her skin. Not until the last word rolled off her tongue did the book change. The pages folded in on themselves and then disappeared entirely.

Medea lowered her wand. "It's done. Exactly as expected."

Isis plucked from the ground the large jewel that had appeared where the book had been. She held it to the light, her fathomless deep-blue eyes wide with wonder. "It's here, inside this jewel."

Circe snatched it from her hand. "Let me see." She turned the jewel in her fingers. "You can turn the pages by rotating the stone. I can read the spells in the right light."

"The spell is reversible," Medea stated confidently. "We can turn it back into the book anytime we need to."

"Which one of us should keep it?" Isis asked.

"Not me," Circe said quickly. "If Mother gave me one sideways look, I'd hand it over immediately."

Medea glanced at Isis.

"You are better at concealing things." Isis shrugged as if the answer was obvious. "I think you should keep it."

Tugging the stone from Circe's fingers, Medea slipped it into her pocket. "Done."

Isis sniffed. "That smell again."

At the sight of Isis's grimace, gooseflesh paraded along Medea's arms even though the temperature was as warm as always. "We did what we came to do. Let's go."

She followed her sisters' hasty retreat into the woods,

but stopped short, just inside the tree line. "The sling. We forgot it in the field."

"That was made from our old baby blankets," Circe said. "Mother and Father will definitely recognize it if they find it."

"Wait here. I'll go." Medea darted toward the field again and swept the blanket off the ground. As she rose from the bed of marigolds, the hair at the base of her neck tingled as if it was trying to stand on end.

Someone was watching her.

She whirled to face the gate again, stared directly through its golden bars at the empty field beyond. There was nothing there. She blinked.

A massive black dragon appeared out of nowhere, staring at her through the gate with shrewd golden eyes that peered from a face of black scales crowned with a set of twisting horns. The beast snorted, studying her. Smoke blew from the curls of its dark nostrils. Fierce. Beautiful.

Enough time passed she was certain the dragon didn't intend to come after her. Steadily, Medea turned on her heel and strode for the cover of the forest.

CHAPTER TWO

I f Tavyss didn't know better, he'd believe the woman was staring straight into his soul. Of course that was complete nonsense. At first she couldn't see him at all. As an immortal dragon shifter, he'd made himself invisible, and few supernatural beings were capable of detecting a dragon cloaked in invisibility. Then again, he'd scented the power coming off her and her sisters even from a distance. Perhaps she was one of the few who could see through his defenses.

Why he'd dropped his invisibility was a bigger mystery. For some reason that bright blue stare made him want to reveal himself. He'd assumed his presence would evoke more of a reaction from her. Only she hadn't looked terrified. On the contrary, she'd stared directly at him with fierce interest before retreating into the garden.

Why was he concerned with how the woman looked at him anyway? His job was to act as the Guardian at the Gate of the Garden of the Hesperides. The only care Tavyss should have had was why the woman was inside the garden to begin with. Only the nymphs who tended the garden were allowed inside, and she didn't look like a nymph. For one thing, she had no gossamer wings, and she was quite a bit bigger than most as well. Not to mention that her skin was far different than the pearlescent complexions of the usual garden inhabitants.

She'd looked human. That couldn't be. He'd never allowed a human through the locked gate. Well, not intentionally. Was it possible someone had slipped inside while he was hunting or sleeping? Not likely. Even if a potential intruder reached the gate, they'd have the goddess's wards to deal with.

There had to be a reasonable explanation. Perhaps Hera had placed the woman there and was aware of her presence.

Hera. He should alert the goddess to what he'd seen. If there were intruders in her garden, she'd want to know immediately. Only, the goddess's bitter heart was hard and black as night. There would be no forgiveness for the one who broke her rules and no leniency for he who failed to keep the intruder out. If someone had snuck inside, she'd likely find a way to punish *him* for it. Worse, if she *had* placed the woman there, she'd taunt him for only now realizing it.

He snorted and dug his claws into the dirt. He couldn't have seen what he thought he'd seen. No one but a god could find this place. The gate was sealed with a magical enchantment. No human was powerful enough to make it past those defenses, especially not a young woman who looked no older than twenty-five.

He blinked. The woman was gone now, having slipped into the forest with the other two, but he continued to stare in her direction.

Hera would want to know about this.

He did not wish to tell her.

No. There was no reason to suffer Hera's wrath when he

wasn't even sure what it was he'd seen. Perhaps the three females were nothing more than oversized nymphs, their wings carefully packed away. Wasn't it more likely that he'd seen a strange, undiscovered type of garden creature than that another supernatural—a witch, elf, human, or shifter like himself—had overcome the many obstacles necessary to break into the garden?

And to think he'd almost brought this to Hera! What a humiliating conversation he'd have suffered had he followed his initial instincts. Clearly he'd seen a nymph, that was all. He shook his head.

Turning, he stretched his wings and looked out over the endless fields of the gods of Olympus. It had been a long time since anyone had challenged him to enter the garden gates, and no one had ever bested him. Only once had a hero and his lover convinced him to help his cause by retrieving a fleece from one of the golden sheep. Even then, the man had never made it inside the garden. The idea was preposterous! Tavyss chuckled, the sound as gritty as embers in his dragon throat.

Although he tried to think of other things, his attention reverted to the spot the woman had vacated. Eventually, with considerable effort, he forced himself to turn away. Enchanting was the only word to describe her. With a grumble, he tried to put her out of his mind. He thought of the sea, but the blue water reminded him of her eyes. Goddess help him, he was practically obsessed.

Clearly the sighting was too much to let go, which meant it was his duty as guardian of the gate to investigate. With a shiver, he shifted into his *soma* form—two legs, two arms—the same form she'd inhabited when he'd spotted her. Although he possessed a set of wings that, if part of her anatomy, she had not revealed. He took to the air and flew over the gate.

He needed to find the woman and ascertain exactly what she was and what she was doing there. It was his duty. His responsibility. Until he was sure, until he'd spoken to her, he was certain he'd never be free of her hold over him.

CHAPTER THREE

"We haven't burst into flames or been swallowed by the earth. You can relax, Circe." Medea waded into the pool at the base of the waterfall, the cool water sending heavenly ripples across her hot, tacky skin. She hadn't mentioned the dragon to her sisters. After all, the beast was on the other side of the gate. Mentioning it would cause her sisters unnecessary worry.

"Thank the gods," Circe said. "Let's not tempt fate again anytime soon."

Isis dove under and broke the surface at the center of the pool. She smoothed her blue-black hair from her forehead. "I'm with Circe on this one. I don't want to go back there again. I thought I'd never clear that scent from my nose."

Medea glided her palms over the surface of the water. "Very well, we won't use the field again. Only I don't think we should practice magic at home anymore. We've already learned the basic spells in the book. Anything we do now will require both space and privacy."

Circe rolled her eyes as if she thought Medea was daft. "Obviously we won't practice at home. Why would we now that the book is manageable? We can use the clearing beside the tanglewood tree."

The tanglewood tree enhanced their power, so much so that the sisters had used branches from its three distinct sections to create their magic wands. As children, when their parents were teaching them basic spells, the clearing beside the tree had served as the perfect place to practice, significantly enriching their experience. But that same reasoning was why the space wouldn't work for them now.

"It's not safe. Mother and Father go there frequently. At least once per day." Medea recalled the blackberry brambles that flourished nearby and drew her mother overmuch.

"The orchard," Isis said. "We can practice between the trees."

"Also forbidden," Medea reminded her.

"Picking the apples is forbidden. Practicing among the trees is not," Isis said.

"I doubt our parents would see it that way," Circe pointed out.

"With any luck, they won't see it at all," Medea said.

Circe waded toward the shore. "Very well; it's a better idea than the field."

Isis swam toward her, the sun sparkling on her darker skin. "We should go before they wonder where we are." She stepped, dripping, onto the beach and pulled her dress over her head. Circe did the same.

"Go on ahead." Medea dipped lower in the water. "I want to soak for a few more minutes. I have an ache in my muscles from the magic."

"You haven't overexerted yourself? Do you need healing?" Circe raised her wand.

"No, I'll be fine. Just a moment in the coolness."

They waved their goodbyes and followed the path away from the lake toward their cottage home. Medea sighed in relief. She'd wanted time alone since they'd performed the spell. *Finally* she could allow herself to think about the dragon. The beast was certainly monstrous with smooth obsidian scales that reminded her of waterworn stone. Although its massive teeth were deadly and prominent, she'd connected with its eyes. Warm golden eyes that sparked with curiosity and intelligence. Her reaction to the Guardian at the Gate was confusing to say the least. Yes, she'd feared the dragon at first. But now that she thought back to her encounter, it hadn't growled or snapped or charged after her. It wasn't fear that made her heart pound now but curiosity.

Leaning back, she allowed her body to float to the surface, the cool water licking her sides. She stared at the branches that arched over the pond. The sun shone through the bright green leaves, warming her skin. The waterfall's rhythmic patter lulled her into pure serenity.

In a blink, two eyes the color of warm honey appeared among the leaves above her, a stranger perched in the branches. A man. Watching her.

A scream tore from her throat. Medea's body caved, sinking into the water with a splash. She kicked violently, swimming to shore as fast as she could. But by the time she'd sprung onto the sandy beach of the pool, pulled on her dress, and reached for her wand in her sleeve pocket, the man was gone.

"Show yourself!" Was she mad or had she actually seen the stranger? Definitely not a nymph, not with his size or his human complexion. What was the spell to reveal what was hidden? She couldn't remember it. Couldn't remember anything.

"I didn't mean to scare you," a deep voice said from the trees.

She searched the branches, but there was nothing there.

"I want to talk."

"Show yourself," she demanded again.

"Lower your wand."

She did as he asked. The man appeared again in the same tree she'd seen him in before, one second gone, the next there. He simply blinked into existence.

"What manner of creature are you?" she asked. She thought he looked like an oversized cat the way he crouched in the branches, his tunic open at the chest.

A strange, tightly coiled tension began low in her abdomen. She'd never seen anything like him. His skin was even darker than Isis's, and it created a stunning presence against the bright blue sky and green tree. She thought she might like to watch him for the rest of the day, perhaps paint his likeness. Having known no other man but her father, she desperately wanted to study the way his muscles might stretch and bunch when he moved.

"I'm coming down."

With her body reacting so strangely to the man, all she could muster was a nod. Two dark wings unfolded from his back, not gossamer like the nymphs who were common in the garden but webbed like a bat's with black scales that reflected gold in the sun. She'd seen that color before. Gilded obsidian. Her mind blanked again as he floated from his perch to the sand in front of her.

"Oh." The sound came from deep inside Medea's throat. Without even thinking about the repercussions, she reached for his wing, longing to touch it, then stopped herself, her hand floating in the air between them. Quickly she retracted it, resting her fingers instead on her stomach.

"Who are you?" she asked. "How is it you came to be in the garden?"

"I came to ask you the same question."

She took a step back, turning her chin away but keeping her eyes on him. "I *live* here. It is you who are new to this place."

He laughed. "I most certainly am not new." He tipped his head. "Although I don't usually come here specifically. I grant you that."

"I've never seen you before," she said defensively. "And I was born in this place and have lived here my entire life."

"You were born in the garden?" One eyebrow peaked, and she was enchanted by the way the corner of his mouth elevated with it.

She nodded. "Yes. Of course. Outsiders are not allowed. Unless you are a god? A friend of Hera's?" She took another step away from him. Strangers were unheard of in the garden, and anyone powerful enough to get in was someone to be feared.

"I am not a god." He paced around her.

He stalked around her like a lithe predator. How distracting he was when he walked, and the sunlight kissed his skin. Her stomach did a funny little flip. She inhaled deeply in response to the feeling and was rewarded with a full breath of his scent: fresh-cut wood, ginger root, and a hint of woodsmoke. Intoxicating! She caught herself leaning toward him before she remembered her good sense.

"Do you always inspect others like this?" She pressed a hand to her quivering stomach. Her words sounded more defensive than she'd intended, but the man flustered her.

"Not always. Just you. What are you?"

"I recall asking you the same thing, and still I have no answer. Are you Hermes, the winged god?"

"I told you I am not a god."

"Then what?"

"Are you a nymph? You don't look like a nymph."

The base of Medea's skull tingled, and her father's warnings screamed in her brain. Technically they were not supposed to be living in the garden. Who was this man who dropped out of the sky? Surely it would not behoove her to tell him the truth. But lying seemed equally risky. She had no idea who he was or what he already knew about her.

"I am no more or less exactly who I am, a lifelong resident of Hera's garden and thankful for my life here."

He smiled, and the sheer radiance of his white teeth and his dimpled cheek made her heart slam against her rib cage. Surely he'd lied. He must be a god with a face like his. He was too perfect to be anything else.

"Now I've told you what I am, I deserve the same respect."

"I..." He hesitated, his eyes roving over her as if he was trying to decide if he should trust her. "I am the Guardian at the Gate. I saw you in the field today and did not recognize your kind."

All her muscles tensed in horror as she realized what he meant. All the signs were there. The amber eyes, the obsidian wings lined with gold. Could this be the transformed dragon? Truly the Guardian at the Gate?

"You are the dragon transformed?" She forced herself to swallow past the lump of fear forming in her throat.

He bowed at the waist. "Although you say you were born here, I've never seen you before this morning. I was unaware any creatures but nymphs lived here."

"We rarely go near the gate, but my sisters wanted to see the flowers."

He rubbed the side of his jaw. "Nymphs rarely spend

time there, but then you are not a nymph, are you?" His tone sounded accusatory, but then his question wasn't a question at all.

Medea licked her lower lip. "I've never had a need to call myself the same or different from the others who live among us. I simply am, as are my sisters."

"Because you were born here." His eyes narrowed and his nostrils flared as he sniffed her. She wondered what she smelled like to him. Probably the waterfall as she'd only now come from swimming in the pool at its base.

"Is that all you wish to know?"

He gave a low growl, his eyes snapping to hers. His chin bobbed in a nod. "I am relieved. For a moment I worried you didn't belong."

She forced a smile. "Doesn't everything belong here? Who could get by you, or through the gate, but perhaps a god?" She looked him over from head to toe. "How is it you look like a man?"

He hesitated a moment as he seemed to contemplate her question. The corner of his mouth twitched, his full lips enchanting her. "I transform into a dragon. I am both, dragon and man."

Medea desperately wanted to see him change, but she knew she was already pushing her luck engaging as she was in this conversation. "I should go." She gestured over her shoulder. "My sisters are waiting for me."

He bowed formally. "Of course. I have distracted you from your activities."

She turned slowly to start down the path but couldn't stop herself from glancing back. How stunning he was, standing there, watching her. "What is your name?"

The question seemed to startle him, as if it was the last thing he presumed she'd ask. "Tavyss," he said. "And yours?"

"Medea." Oh, her parents would be horrified to know she'd given the guardian her true name. She chewed her lip. "It was very nice to meet you. Tavyss."

"You as well," he said. When she turned again to the path, he blurted, "Perhaps we will speak again?"

It was a foolish thing to agree to, but before Medea could stop herself, she met his compelling gaze. "I'd like that very much."

CHAPTER FOUR

E verything about the woman was intriguing. Skin like freshly poured cream, hair the color of a raven's wings. She'd smelled of wild orchids. He'd been entranced by the way the water lapped her sides like a thousand azure tongues as she skimmed across the surface of the pool. How he'd longed to feel what the water had. What must it be like to surround her, to caress her like a wave?

And so over the following weeks, he visited her at her pool time and time again, always careful to wait until her sisters had gone on their way. He wanted her all to himself. Although the reason was still unclear to him, he found her absolutely fascinating.

"Have you come again to guard me, Tavyss?" she'd call to him in the tree.

"It is my duty," he'd respond before dropping down to her side and talking to her for a few precious moments. She was incredibly intelligent and well-read for having spent her life inside the garden, and they would often discuss the legends of the gods or gossip about the garden nymphs.

"You've never told me, Tavyss, do you have family here?"

He rubbed the back of his neck. "I'm alone. I have been for some time."

Her lips flattened in poorly disguised pity. "I don't know what I'd do without my sisters."

With a shrug, he added, "I have a family, but I left them when Hera offered me this position. In truth, I needed somewhere to go, and it was a convenient escape."

"Surely you must have friends among the nymphs," she stated. "Even I have nymphs I speak to regularly. The creatures love to help with daily activities."

"There is one who cleans my cottage, but he has very little to say. His name is Relkin. I think he might be afraid of me."

A ghost of a smile teased beneath her sideways glance. "Just because you turn into a scaled beast with teeth as long as I am tall? The nerve."

"I would never eat a nymph."

She narrowed her eyes, a thought occurring to her. "What do you eat?"

"Sheep. A perk of being the guardian is I'm allowed to hunt the golden sheep."

Her eyebrows shot into her hairline. "It's *you* who takes the sheep? I've wondered since I was a little girl."

"They're what I eat."

"I thought it was forbidden."

"Not for me." He winked at her and took a seat on the branch.

She studied him with her pale blue eyes. What went on inside her lovely head? Medea was an enigma, brave to trust him as she did but also vulnerable. Without claws or sharp teeth, she was utterly defenseless. And didn't that make him surprisingly desperate to protect her?

"Can I ask you something about the sheep?" Her eyes narrowed on his wings.

He nodded.

"Do they taste the same as regular sheep?"

A dimple appeared in his right cheek with his half smile. "There's a metallic aftertaste." He laughed then until his stomach hurt. Sobering, he handed her a book from his personal library. "I brought you a gift."

"*The Saddle of Arythmetes*?" she read off the cover.

Thank the Mountain she could read his language.

"It's a difficult read, to be sure, but one I think you'll find fascinating."

She turned the leather volume in her hands. "Oh? What's it about?"

"This book was written by one of the very first Paragonian philosophers, a famous teacher and dragon shifter named Plintolemy. The story is about a hero named Arythmetes who discovers after a series of challenges in the five kingdoms that each of the communities plays a vital role in sustaining his world. Fairies, elves, dragons, witches, and even vampires are important contributors and only a peaceful coexistence will lead to ultimate prosperity."

She cradled the book in her hands, her blue eyes twinkling with her excitement. "Thank you, Tavyss. I feel like since I've met you, you've opened a door for me. Ironic, considering you guard the gate."

He perused her face, his gaze settling on her mouth. "I feel the same way."

She laughed, bumping her shoulder into his. "But you're on the outside. You can go anywhere you want."

Shaking his head, he stared out over the pool. "I'm not as free as you think."

🦢

Tᴀᴠʏss ʟᴀɴᴅᴇᴅ ᴏᴜᴛsɪᴅᴇ ᴛʜᴇ ɢᴀʀᴅᴇɴ ɢᴀᴛᴇ ᴛʜᴀᴛ ɴɪɢʜᴛ ᴀɴᴅ entered the stone cottage that served as his home, feeling a sense of joy he hadn't experienced in decades. Medea was the reason. Spending time with her woke him up. She saw beauty in the simplest things, things he took for granted. After starting a fire, he watched the flames dance inside the hearth and thought of her until the peacock feather he kept in a glass vase on his hearth began to glow. Then he thought of nothing. He schooled his features and prepared himself for the arrival of the goddess.

"I need your help, dragon." The bright light morphed into the familiar figure of a woman. *Hera.*

Her blond hair and silver-white gown emitted a luminescence that filled the modest cabin. All gods emitted their own light, similar to a star or other celestial body, but Hera's was not a warm, comforting glow. Her light always carried an edge. A threat. A flare before an explosion. Tavyss feared her, and rightly so. Only a fool wouldn't.

"Hera," he said by way of greeting. He fell to his knees and bowed his head. "What is it that brings you into my company?"

"Oh, get up. Aren't we beyond this now?" Her fingers hooked under his chin, and he rose to look her in the eye, then quickly glanced away. Her hands lingered on his face, on his chest. His stomach squirmed at her touch. The sensation was too warm. Too strange. Still, he dared not pull away. One did not intentionally spurn a goddess.

He cleared his throat. "How can I be of service?"

She smoothed his shirt over his chest. "I've recently learned that something very important to me has gone missing." She backed away. "A golden grimoire, a gift from Zeus to atone for an... indiscretion. It was stolen from its protected shrine in the underworld."

"When did this happen?" Tavyss asked. If the theft was recent, he might be able to pick up the scent of the perpetrator.

"Sometime within the past fifty years."

"Fifty years—"

"A blink in the eternity that is our immortal existence, wouldn't you agree?" She folded her arms. "The last time I saw the book was around fifty years ago. Hades notified me it was missing yesterday. When exactly it went missing is anyone's guess."

Tavyss rubbed the back of his neck and the short hair at the base of his skull. He was neither a seer nor a bounty hunter. What did she want from him? "I don't understand. What can I do? It's likely been too long for me to pick up the scent of the thief."

She paced to the other end of the room, gliding her fingers across the back of the single wooden chair he kept there. "I have reason to believe the thief took my book to Ouros."

He shook his head. What would someone from his home world want with her book of spells? Unless it was one of the witches from the kingdom of Darnuith, but the notion that they would both know of the book and have the power to retrieve it seemed unlikely.

"What would lead you to believe such a thing?"

She scowled. "Because the indiscretion my husband was atoning for when he gifted me the grimoire was with the Goddess of the Mountain."

Tavyss inhaled sharply. The Goddess of the Mountain,

Aitna, was the patron goddess of Ouros and the kingdom of Paragon, his homeland. All dragons came from the mountain and returned there if they were killed. Aitna was the goddess of all dragons, their most holy of holies.

"Zeus, you see, gave me the grimoire but gave his lover something as well. My scrying glass will not show me Paragon. I cannot go there. I cannot search the five kingdoms of Ouros for the book myself."

"Do you believe it was Aitna herself who took the book?" Tavyss asked, despite his better judgment. Normally he would not question the goddess, but her accusation was too far-fetched for him not to. "As far as I am aware, she never leaves her mountain."

Hera grunted. "I know not who took it, only that, aside from this garden and Ouros, my looking glass sees all. We both know it's not here in the garden—"

"No, of course not..."

"That leaves only Ouros."

"Are you suggesting I go there to search for it?"

"More than suggesting. You will go and you will find it."

He bowed his head. "Forgive me, but I cannot. I am no longer welcome in Paragon or the Obsidian Palace. If my brother ever knew I had returned to Ouros, he would immediately have me killed. I am a threat to his crown."

She sighed. "Dear Tavyss. I wouldn't ask you to risk your immortal existence if it wasn't entirely necessary."

"You don't understand—I have no power there anymore. I abdicated the throne. My presence... will be distracting and ineffective. I will have no hope of finding your book. The Paragonian regency is even now in transition. My sister will take over the throne from my mother this very year, and my younger brother will rule as co-regent at her side. My presence, as the older sibling, will be viewed as a threat to them despite my renunciation of the crown."

What frustrated him the most was that Hera knew that. When she offered him the position of Guardian at the Gate, he was open about his choice to flee the expectations of Paragon.

"I am aware of the politics of your society." She rolled her eyes toward the ceiling, clearly piqued. "What has this to do with me, dragon?"

"I am only explaining why I cannot be of help to you if the book is truly in Ouros."

She scoffed. "Relax, Tavyss. I wouldn't dream of forcing you to reclaim your birthright and challenge your brother for the throne." She stalked toward him. "I need you here." She stepped close to him, too close, and trailed her nails over his cheek. "All I expect of you is to journey to Paragon and ask your brother or sister for assistance. Surely it will be worth it to them to search for the book in exchange for your leaving Paragon promptly."

A muscle in his jaw twitched over clenched teeth. He'd already made it clear to her that the moment his feet touched Paragonian soil, his life would be at risk. She'd refused to listen, which meant her will was nonnegotiable. Any resistance could end up angering the goddess. Tavyss was a warrior, but he was no match for Hera. "If it pleases you, I can deliver this message and make the request, although I will not be able to search for the book myself without raising their ire and suspicion."

She pressed her lips against his cheek, close to his mouth. His skin crawled with the tingling heat she left there. Her scent was too sweet, almost cloying. It was all he could do to disguise his disgust.

"It pleases me," she purred.

"Then I will go." He broke away from her and crossed to the door. "Give me a few days' time to make a plan for securing a formal audience with my siblings."

"Very well, dragon," she said, drumming her fingers on her upper arm. "I'm counting on you."

CHAPTER FIVE

"M edea!"

Medea jerked as the water she was pouring into Isis's jug overflowed the spout and ran onto her sister's fingers. "Sorry," she mumbled.

Isis shook the excess water off and gave her a quizzical look. "What has gotten into you today?"

"What? Nothing. I'm fine." No way could Medea explain to Isis that her brain kept dwelling on a set of gold eyes and black wings. Tavyss was a delicious secret, a dark dream that brought a few moments of heart-pounding excitement into her day.

"Isis is right," Circe declared. "You've been distracted all morning. Father asked you what you wanted for breakfast and you said yes."

Isis giggled. "It wasn't a yes or no question, Medea."

With a shrug, Medea said, "Tired, I guess."

"You'd better get your head on straight before we practice our magic. You'll end up setting something on fire." Isis flashed a dark smile.

Her sister was right, she did need to clear her head. Medea always read the spells, Isis performed any work with symbols or stones, and Circe worked with plants, roots, and potions. They each had their role, and if one of them was distracted, their spell fell apart.

The only problem was that Medea seemed to have no control over her fleeting thoughts. She hadn't stopped thinking about Tavyss since the last time they'd met beside the waterfall. He'd thoroughly captivated and charmed her.

She longed to tell her sisters about him but hesitated. Circe and Isis were her only friends, and they'd always shared everything, but if she told them about Tavyss, would they worry about the repercussions? She'd been the one to convince them to do the spell in the marigold field. If they found out that the Guardian at the Gate had been watching them, a dragon who'd suddenly taken interest in who they were and had the power to reveal their existence to Hera, would they ever trust her again? Could they possibly fathom what he'd come to mean to her these past weeks?

"Are you coming? The faster we get this water back to the house, the sooner we can practice!" Circe strode down the path toward the cottage, looking utterly frustrated.

Medea stood slowly from the pool and sidled up to Isis, who was waiting for her, a dark glint in her eye.

"Now you must tell me the truth. What is so distracting, sister?"

"I didn't sleep well last night," Medea murmured.

"This is more than lack of sleep." Isis raised an eyebrow.

After a moment's hesitation, Medea asked, "Have you ever wondered about men?"

"Men?" Isis frowned. "Like the human men from our books?"

"Men like father but our age," Medea said. "Men who might want to be with us like Father is with Mother."

"There are no men in the garden," Isis said flatly. "Unless you have taken a liking to one of the male nymphs, but their bodies are strange, Medea. I don't think they'd be physically compatible—"

"I'm not attracted to a male nymph, Isis!" Medea exclaimed. "I'm simply asking, hypothetically, have you ever thought about men?"

They ducked into the cottage and left their jugs near the hearth for their mother before all three of them ventured out toward the hills on the far side of the garden.

"I've thought about men," Circe whispered when they were far enough away from home to feel alone. Medea hadn't realized she'd even heard their conversation. "After we conjured the grimoire, I wondered if we could conjure mates in the same way. I think I would like to know a man."

Isis's dark brows rose. "You want to conjure a man? What if you try and accidentally summon a beast or an ugly slob who paws at you incessantly?"

Circe laughed. "What if he's a prince? I'd like to kiss a prince."

They arrived at the hillside where the golden sheep roamed. The round balls of gold fluff wandered away from them as they neared, their lips never leaving the emerald grasses on which they grazed.

"Anyway," Medea said. "I can't stop obsessing over the idea that Mother and Father didn't think it through. Yes, we are safe here in the garden, but we are alone. We are forever children, never to know love or the feel of a man."

A shadow passed through Isis's expression. "Only if we stay forever."

They all stared at each other, all levity draining from their features. Leaving the garden was something they never spoke of. But wasn't that why they'd conjured the book to begin with? They'd been frightfully interested in learning what was out there. They wanted to exceed their parents' abilities and needed a teacher from the outside.

Medea pulled out the gem that held the golden grimoire and held it up to the light. "Considering we don't particularly want to risk summoning a pawing slob, what shall we practice today?"

"I'd like to fly," Circe said.

Medea laughed. "Fly?"

Isis shrugged. "We've levitated many things of all shapes and sizes. Why not ourselves?"

The pages flipped like a kaleidoscope inside the facets as Medea turned the gem. She focused her intention on their goal—flight. Her mind immediately jumped to Tavyss and his wings. The pages stopped flipping.

"Here's one." She handed the gem to Isis.

"Transformation?" Isis shot her an incredulous glance. "Instead of magical levitation, you wish to give us wings?"

Circe snatched the stone from Isis's hands. "Will the wings actually work?"

"Only for as long as the spell is active. It's not permanent."

Isis's smile held a hint of madness. "Let's do it."

One by one they committed the spell to memory, formed a circle, and began. Isis used mud to trace symbols on her sisters' shoulder blades with her finger and shifted to allow Circe to draw the same pattern on her own. Isis drew the same symbol on the earth to act as an anchor. At Medea's request, Circe collected and mixed a concoction of herbs that each of them drank despite its foul odor. Then Medea sang the book's incantation.

Dark gossamer wings sprang from Isis's back first, followed by Circe's and finally Medea's. The three sisters bounced, giddy with excitement.

"We've done it!" Isis pushed off into the air, flapping her new wings and delighting in their capabilities.

Medea took a mighty leap, the muscles of her back straining as she dipped and soared with her sisters over the grazing sheep. After some time, she broke from her sisters and coasted over the tops of the trees, hoping to find Tavyss at their usual meeting place.

Joy seized her heart when she found him crouched, waiting in the same tree where she'd first seen him. Warmth blossomed inside her at the sight, as if her spirit had lit a candle inside her chest. Heart fluttering, she flew from behind him and landed on the same branch.

His arm slammed into her gut and turned her effortlessly on the tree branch, thrusting her up against the trunk. The move was so quick, so practiced, she found herself too breathless to make a sound. She stared up at him. Her heart hammered, jarred into action by fear but also something else, something she couldn't quite name.

"Medea?" His eyes drifted over her face and the wings. He loosened his grip but planted his hands on either side of her shoulders, caging her in. The heat of his nearness warmed her through her thin dress.

"It's me," she said, overwhelmed by his strength and presence.

His dark wings lorded over his shoulders, shading her. There was a talon as long as her hand at the tip of each one, and she couldn't help but think how easily he could tear her apart if he wanted to. Thank all the gods she did not believe he wanted to. Even now recognition was dawning and his expression softening.

His dark eyes traced the length of her wings. "I didn't know you could fly."

Their gazes locked, and Medea's lower abdomen filled with a strange and weighty need. Any fear she'd felt before was jarred loose by a powerful wave of heat that warmed her cheeks. Her skin tingled. She swallowed hard and felt her lids flutter at the intensity between them.

She wiggled her temporary wings. "I... I guess I'm full of surprises."

He blinked those arresting golden eyes and retreated along the broad branch of the tree. "I wanted to see you again."

That admission made her stomach quiver, and she shifted on the branch, her blood racing when their eyes met. Her tongue felt thick as she responded. "I hoped to see you again too. These meetings, they're becoming a habit."

His impossibly full lips twitched, and he peered at her from under half-lowered lids. "I hope I didn't scare you. I didn't know it was you."

She braced her hands on the trunk behind her. "I was startled, but I don't feel I'm in any danger with you. After all, aren't you here to guard me?"

"It is my duty." He blessed her with the full force of his smile.

"I feel safer already." She glanced down at the water below them and then back up at him, but the warm ache he inspired didn't lessen in the least. "Where did you learn to do that? You moved so fast. Had I been an enemy, I would have surrendered immediately."

His expression grew serious. "I trained as a warrior since

my youth. It is the way of my people, and it's why Hera asked me to guard the gate."

That surprised her. She'd assumed he'd always been here. A creation of the gods. "You're not from here? I mean, originally?"

"No. In fact that book I gave you, *The Saddle of Aryth-metes*, it is from my home world."

"You're from Paragon?" It made sense now, but she'd never put it together.

He inclined his head. "Medea... do you mind that I come to see you as often as I do? It has been a long time since I've had... a friend, if I can call you that, and I find myself in need of one today."

She licked her bottom lip, the smile fading from her face as she digested his words. "I'm glad you came. And I am your friend. I've enjoyed our meetings more than I can say."

He glanced down at the rippling pool. "If I tell you something, can you keep my secret?"

"The Guardian at the Gate has a secret? I'm intrigued."

"I am serious, Medea. You can tell no one. Not even your sisters." He shook his head.

"I won't tell anyone." She sensed now the gravity of his secret and reached across the branch to take his hand in hers. Touching him was far better than looking at him. Heat radiated from his skin and seemed to travel through her body, hot enough to melt the top off a box full of butterflies that now fluttered madly inside her. She tried not to fixate on the smooth edge of his jaw. "You can trust me, Tavyss. I can see something is bothering you. Tell me."

He squeezed her hand. "I wasn't always the Guardian at the Gate. Before... in Paragon... I was supposed to be king."

She blinked rapidly, her gaze snapping from his mouth to his eyes. "Excuse me, did you say *king*?"

He stared at their coupled hands. "I am the eldest heir to the kingdom of Paragon on a world called Ouros. I was destined to rule as co-regent alongside my sister."

"But... but then why are you here? Why aren't you ruling your kingdom?"

"I didn't want to be king." With one hand, he rubbed his eyes and frowned. "No, that's not exactly true. I didn't want to rule with my sister. Eleanor is cruel and vicious. You've never known a viler person." His lips tightened into a scowl. "She and my younger brother took turns making my life a living hell in the palace. The idea of ruling by her side for two thousand years per our custom made me long to give up my immortality just to escape the obligation. It felt more like a prison sentence than my destiny."

She rubbed her thumb over his hand. "You agreed to help Hera here, to escape your destiny?"

He nodded. "As my coronation drew near, I ran away. Left Paragon and traveled to a remote island north of the five kingdoms." He shook his head. "You have no idea what I'm talking about, do you?"

"I do! I've read the book you gave me. The five kingdoms of Ouros are Paragon, Darnuith, Everfield, Nochtbend. I don't remember the last one."

"Rogos, the kingdom of the elves."

His long lashes fluttered in the most mesmerizing way, and thankfully he changed course. "I met Hera on an island called Kryptos, north of Paragon, in the realm of the gods. She offered me an escape. I have food, a home, a nymph who sews and cleans for me, work. And I am free from the expectations of my birth."

"If this is what you wanted, what vexes you now? Or are you trying to woo me with your title?" She arched a brow.

The dimple was back, and his amber eyes twinkled

mischievously. "I believe I would like to woo you, Medea, but you don't strike me as the type to be moved easily. I do not believe wealth or prestige would suit your fancy."

A smile spread her lips wide. How could he know her so well already? "I've never had any use for either."

"No, you wouldn't have. But then what would woo you? What do you dream about at night when you are alone?"

His burning gaze slowly raked down her body, and she thought she might combust at the answering heat it produced in her.

"Knowledge," she admitted. "If there is one thing I value, it is knowledge. My experience in this garden is so limited. Indeed, I cherish my time with you. You always... take me away from this place."

"Then I will continue to share my stories and pray I further garner your affection."

Medea paused, squeezing his hand. "What was it you were saying before? I find you utterly distracting."

He offered her a half smile. "The feeling is mutual." A pained look crossed his face. "Hera has asked me to go back to Paragon, to look for something she's lost. I cannot refuse her."

"You seem reluctant."

"I am dreading it. I want nothing to do with my sister Eleanor or my younger brother Brynhoff. I fear my siblings will not take kindly to my visit. They will assume I've returned for the crown, and they will most definitely attempt to remove the competition."

Medea's heart thudded uncomfortably at the implied threat. "Do you mean they might... become violent?"

"There is nothing my sister would like better than to see my head on a pike."

The awful thought caused Medea's chest to tighten. She

hadn't experienced much violence and couldn't imagine such a family. She squeezed his hand and urged him to continue.

"I'm a fair warrior in my world," he explained. "Neither one of them could defeat me in one-on-one combat, but they have the benefit of each other, not to mention rule over the Obsidian Guard—that's the royal army of the kingdom of Paragon. I no longer have any standing in the royal court. They could have me executed on a whim."

The thought filled Medea with the darkest form of dread. "You simply can't go then," she blurted.

He barked a hard laugh. "I'm afraid even a dragon must obey a goddess if he wants to avoid a very uncomfortable situation."

"You mean having your head on a pike here rather than there." Tears welled in her eyes when he affirmed her suspicions. She couldn't even think of Tavyss being in such danger. He was her friend, and she absolutely must do something to help him.

"Medea? Medea?" Her sisters called to her from the woods.

"I must go...," she said. "My sisters will wonder where I am."

He dropped her hand, looking dejected. "I understand. I've taken too much of your time today. Thank you for your kind ear."

"Don't be silly. I hope you will be back tomorrow." She beamed up at him.

"I cannot put off Hera's mission for long."

"Tavyss, before you go to Paragon, will you see me again? Tomorrow in the orchard? I may have something that will help you." Medea squeezed his arm and prayed he'd give the plan that was formulating in her brain a chance before he put himself at risk.

He spread his wings. "You've already helped me. Believe me, listening is likely all anyone could do."

"Please," she said. "Tomorrow. In the orchard."

He gave her a dashing smile. "I'd consider it an honor."

CHAPTER SIX

Although it was risky to delay doing Hera's bidding, Tavyss decided to wait to go to Paragon, in no small part because of Medea. He doubted she could actually help him in any way with his problem, but he couldn't say no to another meeting with her. She was a mystery, an enigma. Yesterday he'd discovered she *did* have wings like a nymph, and she'd said she was born in the garden, but she was unlike any creature he'd ever known. Unique. Special.

When he did go to Paragon, if Eleanor and Brynhoff had their murderous way, he might never see her again. He'd make the most of his last hours here and tell her what she meant to him. After, he'd hand himself over to his fate.

The next afternoon, he spread his wings and soared over the orchard, its golden apples sparkling like a galaxy of stars in the sunlight. He smiled when he saw her, but his excitement turned into something more. His body reacted as it never had before, and his mind flashed back to when she was naked, floating on the water. His dragon coiled and chuffed. A gritty inner voice whispered, *Mine*.

The dragon's claim surprised him. It was no small thing

for a dragon to take an interest in a potential mate. Among his kind, mating bonds were sacred and permanent. Dragons who bonded and somehow lost their mates were known to beg for death rather than live after that holy link was severed.

Which meant, at least to his inner dragon, Medea had become far more than a friend. He wanted her. He could not deny it. For his dragon to wish to bond with her, that was far more serious and more dangerous.

Below him, he spotted the three sisters. Angry words reached his ears, and he silently came to rest on a branch, making himself invisible to avoid notice. He focused all his attention on the argument happening below him.

"Since when do you need time alone?" Circe asked. Medea spoke of her often and he deduced it was her based on her lighter complexion.

Medea crossed her arms over her chest. "It will help all of us. I want to get in touch with my personal magic. Meditate. Study and practice."

"We've always practiced together," Isis protested, her darker skin and eyes his clue to her identity. "Where is this coming from? Where did you go yesterday afternoon?"

There was a long pause. Medea cast her gaze around her. Was she looking for him? She fisted her hands and punched straight down at her sides. "I've made a friend. A male friend."

Circe and Isis looked at each other in wide-eyed wonder.

"What kind of male friend?" Isis asked.

"Is he a nymph?" Circe added, pursing her lips.

Medea shook her head. "He's a... dragon."

The two sisters' dual expressions of astonishment must have hit Medea hard, because she crossed her arms against them. "He turns into a man. A man... with wings."

"But... how?" Isis shook her head. "Where did he come from?"

"He guards the gate." Medea sighed heavily, her shoulders slumping. "He saw us that afternoon in the marigold field."

She closed her eyes against the onslaught of sharp language they flung her way.

Tavyss was tempted to reveal himself. The urge to protect Medea was almost undeniable. Listening to them attack her and not intervening was torture, and he balled his hands into fists. But if there was one incontrovertible truth about Medea, it was that she loved her sisters. If he revealed himself, he couldn't ensure things wouldn't get complicated, and he'd never forgive himself for hurting ones that she loved.

"No, Medea! You cannot be friends with this male. He could—"

She raised her hand to Circe and shook her head. "I told him about us... that we were born here in the garden. He's understanding and kind. He won't hurt you."

The sisters exchanged glances.

"He was accepting?" Circe asked.

"Very... accepting." Medea smiled then. "He's kind and handsome. The power he puts off, I can feel it. It makes my skin tingle."

Above her, Tavyss couldn't stop himself from grinning until his cheeks hurt. She thought he was handsome. He leaned in, hoping she'd say more.

Circe brushed her fingertips over her bottom lip. "Truly?"

"Yes. But you must leave now. He is supposed to meet me here, soon, at this very hour."

Isis and Circe exchanged glances before finally seeming

to cave to Medea's plea. Isis offered up a wicked smile. "Very well, sister, we will leave you to your male *friend*, but we expect a full report."

"Agreed." The tension in Medea's shoulders seemed to ease as her sisters left the clearing and traveled down the path toward the pool.

Tavyss dropped his invisibility and soared down to Medea. "Thank you for saying those things about me."

Medea frowned. "I didn't know you were there."

"I... I am sorry. I should not have listened in on your private conversation, but I came to see you and overheard—"

She waved a hand dismissively. "Then you know that yes, I told them about you. I hope that was okay. You never asked me to keep your existence a secret."

He smiled, relieved that he hadn't stoked her anger with his eavesdropping. She actually seemed more distraught that he might be displeased with her for telling her sisters about him.

"I am happy you told them about me." He tucked a lock of her hair behind her ear. "Then they won't be surprised when I seek you out again."

"Have you come to guard me again?" She giggled.

"It's my solemn duty." He held out his hand to her. "Will you walk with me? I love the orchard at this time of day. The apples look like stars."

"I'd love to."

He led her between the trees, and hand in hand, they fell into step.

"I think I have an answer to your problem." Medea fidgeted with the skirt of her dress as if whatever she had to tell him made her nervous.

Tavyss forced his expression to remain impassive. Whatever solution she planned to offer might be simple, given her limited view of the world, but he planned to be contemplative and respect her idea anyway. Whatever it was, he'd consider it.

"What if you could send a message to Paragon without physically going there?"

"Do you mean by bird or... Hermes?" He chuckled at that. The messenger god would likely not take up this cause. His dislike of Hera was well known.

"My family and I are different than others in this garden." Medea glanced down at her feet.

Her fingers continued to fidget, and her forehead wrinkled with what could only be worry. Now he was beyond curious. What could make her so anxious?

"Yes. I've noticed. It's what drew me to you. When I saw you in the field, you were so different I thought you didn't belong."

Her petal-pink tongue licked along her bottom lip, almost driving him to distraction. "We can do magic. Strong magic like a witch."

"How is it you know the magic of witches?" he asked tentatively.

She did not answer but released his hand to tangle her fingers in front of her hips. "I believe, if you'll let me, that I can project you to your sister on the astral plane. Your consciousness will be there, but you will remain safely here."

"Astral projection?" His brows sank low until he thought he might give himself a headache from the tension in his forehead. She was serious. "Have you done this before?"

"Sort of." Her eyes rolled toward the heavens. "Yes. Although only with myself, not carrying another person. I'm sure that I am capable of it though."

He studied her features. "You're serious?"

"As a stone." She tucked her hair behind her ears.

"Where did you learn this magic?" he demanded.

Her lips flattened into a thin line. "My people are born with it." If there was more to it, she didn't elaborate.

As he searched her face, he came to the conclusion that, although he believed her, he'd have to experience this magic to deduce its true potency. Truly, until he did, he was afraid to examine her claims too closely.

She slipped her hand into his and continued walking along the center of the orchard.

It wasn't long before he'd made up his mind. "If you can do it, I would like to try."

CHAPTER SEVEN

W hen Tavyss smiled, it was as if the sun had risen
and shone warm upon her face. Medea led him to
a mossy patch between the trees. He trusted her. To put his
problem into her hands as he had showed a respect for her
that she hadn't fully expected. She'd braced herself for a full
interrogation about her powers and their origins, but he
hadn't pursued it. A strange thought wormed its way into
her mind that perhaps he didn't want to know.

"Sit here." She gestured toward a patch of moss, then sat
cross-legged across from him. Reaching into her pocket, she
removed the gem, held it up to her eye, and turned it.

"What is that stone? It looks like a diamond." He
reached for it.

Laughing, she pulled it out of his reach and guided his
hand back down to his leg.

"I need it to complete this spell. Now, do you wish to talk
about a stone or do this magic?"

"The magic." He slanted a smile in her direction. "For
now."

Gently, she released his hand and brought the stone to

her eye again. "Ah, there it is." She noted the spell, repeating its steps in her head until she knew them by heart, then slipped the gem back into her pocket. Reaching into her sleeve, she drew her wand.

Tavyss eyed the wand skeptically. "Will this hurt, Medea?"

"No. I will not hurt you." Touching his cheek, she met his amber eyes. She hoped she was telling the truth. She'd never performed this spell before. It shouldn't hurt, but how could she be sure?

Wrapping his hand around hers, he pressed a kiss to her palm. "Then I am ready when you are."

Her skin burned where his lips had touched. Oh, how she longed to know what it would feel like for that kiss to have been on her mouth. But she couldn't think about that now because she needed to make sure that Tavyss was around long enough to someday, maybe, kiss. She leaned back, focused on him, on the land of his youth, which she'd studied for hours by candlelight the night before, and spoke the incantation.

"*Ekdiókontai*," she cried, circling the wand above her head before pointing it straight at him.

A pulse of energy poured out of her and washed over him like a wind. His eyes went blank. A blue halo surrounded his body. She felt him go, felt his soul cast out toward Paragon, led by his thoughts, his memories. The connection between them tightened like a drawn rope until she had to lean back against the invisible force.

And then she waited.

And waited.

And waited.

The sun arced overhead and began to descend. Sweat bloomed on her upper lip. Ready or not, she'd have to pull

Tavyss back soon or she'd pass out from overusing her power. She wasn't sure what would happen if she did, and she was afraid to find out.

Thankfully, the pull between them slackened and she pitched forward, reeling in the magical thread that held them together. She gasped as he landed back inside his body and collapsed into her arms. His weight was too much to bear, and she rolled onto her back, his body pinning her to the moss.

"Tavyss? Tavyss, I can't breathe."

He blinked at her. Finally he seemed to notice where he was and rolled off her and onto his back with a groan. She sat up slowly and leaned over him. He didn't move.

"Are you all right? Did it work?" she asked. "You were gone for hours."

His expression gave nothing away as his eyes roved, then locked onto hers. With a noticeable amount of effort, he propped himself on his elbows. Unexpectedly, his hand shot out and hooked behind her neck.

"Oh—!" Her sound of surprise was cut short when his lips met hers. He kissed her with a white-hot passion she had never experienced, never even dreamed of.

His lips burned against her own, a wicked and wonderful fire that she drank in. She'd read about kissing, but all the books in the world couldn't have prepared her for this. His mouth was sultry and wet, like a firm peach warmed in the sun, and she tasted him, welcoming his tongue against her own. She breathed in his smoky-wood scent and gave herself over to the flutter of energy that rose within her.

The things that kiss did to her! As exhausted as she was from performing the spell, her heart galloped in wild fits. The world sharpened as if all the sensations she'd ever experienced were concentrated into the place where their mouths joined. Her stomach flitted like birds flushed from the trees. Lower still, the place between her thighs ached with need. She was falling, dropping from the sky toward him. Everything vibrated and whooshed inside her until she was left breathless and her head spun. When he finally broke the kiss, she was left gasping.

"It worked, Medea," he said, pulling her into his arms. "Your spell worked."

CHAPTER EIGHT

A s Tavyss held Medea in his arms, somewhere in the back of his mind he understood that she was too powerful to belong in the garden. He'd believed her when she said she was born there. The acrid scent of a lie would be impossible for her to hide from his dragon senses. But she didn't belong there. Of that he was sure.

His latest theory was that a god or goddess had planted her there, perhaps as a way to exact revenge against Hera. The affairs of the gods were notoriously tumultuous, and Hera was not well liked among her kind. The goddess held a reputation for bitterness and a vengeful nature. One of Zeus's many past lovers might have proudly done the deed.

But Tavyss couldn't bring himself to care anymore. However Medea had arrived, the power she'd displayed today, conducting his spirit to Paragon, marked her as a witch—a very powerful one. He was aware of no other crea-ture who could wield such magic other than a god. He'd go so far as to say that she was as strong as any witch he'd ever known.

That should have concerned him. If Hera found out a

witch was living in her garden, she'd see her as a threat and expect Tavyss to eliminate her. Which was precisely why he hadn't asked Medea what she was. He cared too much about her. Hell, his inner dragon wanted her. Plus what he didn't know for certain, he had no obligation to tell Hera.

Medea's magic had been a godsend. Once he'd reached Paragon, he'd appeared to his sister Eleanor in her chambers, and although she'd immediately attempted to take off his head, her claws had passed right through him. That got her attention. He'd conveyed Hera's message slowly and carefully, along with a threat that if the golden grimoire could not be found, there would be repercussions from the gods. Eleanor had assumed that his astral projection was courtesy of Hera and thus agreed to assign her best people to finding the grimoire.

All that and now he was back in Medea's arms. The deed was done. He might as well have returned to the bosom of heaven itself.

"I've never been kissed before." Medea brushed her fingertips lightly across her lips.

He reached for her and ran his fingers along the edge of her raven-dark hair. She reminded him of a warm night, her skin as luminescent as the stars and her hair flowing like the celestial sky around her shoulders.

"I find myself drawn to you, Medea." He swallowed. "Drawn to you like I haven't been drawn to anyone in... ever. I think about you always."

Her lips parted, her breath hitching in her throat. "I think about you also."

He reached for her again. Her eyes sparkled mischievously as she offered up her mouth to him. This time the kiss moved deeper. He slid her onto his lap, burying his hands in the dark silk at the back of her head.

"What's that?" She drew back.

He heard it now too, and his cheeks heated with awareness at the deep rumble in his chest. "My mating trill. It seems my inner dragon finds you irresistible."

"I like it, although it's hard to believe that the massive beast I saw outside the gate is somehow inside you." She rested her ear against his chest, her hot breath warming his nipple through his tunic. Even if he'd wanted to hide his true feelings for her, he couldn't have suppressed the resulting purr. His body's response to her was like the wagging tail of a dog. Instinctual. Immediate. She sent fire through his veins.

He gathered her hair in his hands and brushed his lips against her ear. "I am the dragon. In some ways, my beast is more me than this form. That part of me though tends to think in more simple terms. When my inner dragon is hungry, he eats, when thirsty, he drinks, and when he wants a woman, wants her to be *his*, forever...."

"Forever?"

"My feelings for you run deep. Maybe deeper than you are ready to hear."

Her cheeks pinked. Twisting in his lap, she locked her eyes on his, bottomless pits of blue under heavy lids. "I think I feel what your dragon wants."

How could she not? He was as hard as iron under her. His hand drifted along her back and around her bottom. Encouraged by her soft sound of contentment, he rubbed languid circles there, grazing the tips of his fingers along the space between her thighs.

"Have you cast a spell on me, Medea? I find myself enthralled by you. More deeply so than ever in my years."

Her lips caressed his, and he felt her smile against his

teeth. "You've caught me. I've used all my witchy wiles to ensnare you, and now you are mine."

Mine. His dragon coiled and stretched inside his skin at the word. But Tavyss's logical mind snagged on a different one. *Witchy.* Did Medea know what she was? Did she realize she was a witch?

He opened his mouth to ask her about it but was cut off by the deep sound of a man's voice calling her name. She scrambled off him. "I must go."

"Why? Who is that?"

"My father," she said. "It's late. I haven't done my chores." She started toward the sound, but he grabbed her wrist.

"Tomorrow? Here again?"

She raised her eyebrows. "I'm not sure when I'll be able to get away."

"Then I will watch for you all day," he whispered sincerely.

"Tomorrow." She nodded. Her fingers slipped from his and she was gone.

Tavyss returned to his cottage, plucked the peacock feather from its vase, and waited as it glowed to life between his fingers. The sooner he told Hera he'd done as she asked, the sooner she would leave him alone to his own pursuits. Bright light blinded him, and then she was there, as strange and irritating as ever.

"Hera." He returned the feather to the vase, then bowed to the goddess.

"Why do you call me here, dragon?"

"Only to tell you that I did as you commanded. My sister

Eleanor has agreed to task the Obsidian Guard with finding your book. If the golden grimoire is anywhere in the five kingdoms, she will locate it."

"You please me, dragon." She swaggered closer, her gaze drifting toward his mouth. "Come closer. Allow me to reward you for your efforts."

She leaned in as if to kiss him, but he pulled away. It wasn't a conscious decision. If he'd been thinking at all, he would have held extremely still, as a mouse caught in the predatory gaze of a cat, and hoped she lost interest. As it was, his retreat only incited her and she glared at him, the muscles around her mouth tightening.

"Why do you recoil from me?"

Desperate to concoct a story she'd believe, he stared into the fire. "I am worthy of no reward, goddess. My only desire is to serve you."

"Oh, but I have many desires, and there are many ways you can serve me." Her fingers traced a line from his ear to the tip of his chin.

"I regret I am unable to... aid you in that way."

She drew her hand back and crossed her arms in a huff. "Why not? Do you not find me comely?"

"I do, it's just—"

"Then what is it?" she asked through gritted teeth.

"I am mated," he blurted.

Her blue eyes turned cold as ice, and rage danced in the corners of her expression.

"I can't control it. A mated dragon is unable to... perform with anyone other than their mate. The bond is too strong."

"I'm familiar with the customs of your kind. What I am unfamiliar with is this mate you speak of. You've never mentioned her before. You were not mated when I brought you here." She raised a brow.

He closed his eyes and chided himself for entertaining Hera's advances when he'd first arrived. They'd never gone so far as to become lovers, but there had been unspoken promises in their flirtation, possessiveness in her touch. He licked his lips. She would know if he lied.

"It happened when I returned to Paragon." Not a lie. His dragon had voiced his claim on Medea at the time she'd projected his ghost to the Obsidian Palace.

"Who is she?" the goddess asked through clenched teeth.

He sighed. This wasn't going to be easy. "No one of importance. Not a goddess. Not a princess. Just a girl who happened upon a dragon who cannot forget her."

Hera grunted in disgust. "Typical," she murmured. The goddess rolled her eyes. "Bring me the book as soon as you have it. Come directly to me, do you understand?"

He swallowed. "Yes. If my siblings find it, I will bring it to you."

The goddess glowed brighter and bared her teeth. "She'd better find it, dragon. Do not misunderstand me. I'm tasking you with this, and I will not be appeased until I have it."

A muscle in his jaw tightened to the point of pain. "Yes, goddess."

CHAPTER NINE

"What was it like?"

Medea lowered her chin and gave Isis a secret smile.

Both of her sisters were huddled with her at the base of the tanglewood tree, desperate for information. They'd witnessed the kiss from behind the cover of a large tree in the apple grove. She should have known they would. There was absolutely nothing more exciting in any of their lives as a man in their midst. She couldn't deny them the information they sought so ardently.

"The kiss was warm and soft." Her cheeks heated as she remembered it. "But his body was hard. Hard everywhere, like the muscles of your calves. And his skin was hot like he'd been standing by a fire. That's because he's a dragon. They run hotter than the rest of us."

"What about his...?" Circe raised an eyebrow.

"Circe!" Isis elbowed her in the arm.

"More than adequate," Medea said with an impish grin. "Everything we've read about as far as I could tell. I mean, we didn't..."

"We know." Circe sighed and gave her a wicked wink. "Although how you managed to stop, I can't imagine. You must have been as curious as we are."

"There was so much more than what I expected. My heart pounded in my chest, and a sweat broke out across my skin like when we were children playing chase. Something else, a connection. I felt it snap into place between us, almost like we were meant for each other. I think he's my destiny."

Isis stifled a laugh. "What do you mean, your destiny?"

"Like how we were destined to be sisters, and Mother and Father were destined to be our parents. He is my future, my next family."

"Like Mother and Father?" Circe inclined her head.

"I think so." Medea pulled her knees into her chest and wrapped her arms around them. "If he feels the same way. He might not. How does one know for sure? I have no experience with this love magic."

"Only..." Isis's dark eyes narrowed, and her fingers pressed into her bottom lip.

"What sister?"

Isis released a tightly held breath. "He doesn't know who you are, not really. He doesn't know our story. No one can love a lie."

Medea's heart sank, and a stone formed in the pit of her stomach at the word. Had she, despite her efforts not to, deceived Tavyss?

"Nonsense. What does he think she is?" Circe tossed up her hands. "Nymphs don't do magic. After this long, he must suspect that Medea is a witch, and if he doesn't, it's his fault for not using his head."

"No, Circe, Isis is right. I've misled him in the most awful way." A wave of guilt crashed into Medea as the truth of the matter became crystal clear. Her voice hitched. "He's the Guardian at the Gate, and we are here without Hera's permission. He doesn't know everything about our parents or what we are. I... I have to tell him the entire truth. If I don't, someday he'll find out, and then everything we've built will be torn to shreds. When I see him this afternoon, I must explain it all to him."

"You're seeing him again? Today?" Isis grinned.

"Yes, and this time please give us privacy. If I have to use a spell, I will." The glare Medea gave her sisters showed she was serious.

"Fine," Circe said. Isis reluctantly bowed her head in agreement. "But I want to hear everything when it's over."

MEDEA WAITED IN THE GROVE, SURROUNDED BY GOLDEN APPLE trees, as the sun began to set and the fuchsia light glinted off the metallic fruit. Tavyss arrived in the blink of an eye, his wings still outstretched from flight, his gaze reaching for her.

"You came," she said.

His golden gaze locked onto her, and her insides seemed to melt under the warm honey. "I couldn't wait to see you."

He strode toward her. At first she thought he meant to take her into his arms and kiss her again. But then he stopped short, his expression hard to read, and took a seat beside her on the mossy knoll.

Should she tell him now about who she really was? Their eyes locked and her stomach gave a delicious flutter that sent a bloom of sparks through her insides. She glanced away, unable to work up the courage to go through with it.

"Have you ever wondered what they taste like?" she

asked, glancing up toward the golden apples. "The nymphs who gather the fallen ones say that if you eat the fruit, it can kill you. They say it holds too much power and destroys you from within."

Tavyss snorted. "Centuries tending this garden and they've never taken a bite."

"It's forbidden! If they want to remain here, they have to follow Hera's rules."

"Hera is a narcissist who would rather her fruit rot on the ground than someone else enjoy it."

Medea gasped and looked over both shoulders. "Shhh. You shouldn't say such things. What if she's listening?"

He leaned back on his elbows and stared up at the sky. "She never comes here."

"How do you know?"

"Because I know her." He picked the side of his nail. "She gave me the job of guarding the gate after all."

"Then if you know her, why doesn't she ever come here?"

"This garden was a gift from Gaea on her wedding day to Zeus. He treats her like dirt. The god has never been faithful and largely ignores her now. This garden is a reminder of everything she was promised on the day she was wed that never came to fruition," he said.

"How sad. Can't she live her own life since he's obviously living his?"

"Oh, she tries. The problem is no man, certainly no god, would risk angering Zeus by being with her. She's a lonely, angry, and bitter goddess. Those nymphs are right to fear her, but the truth is that the apples are harmless."

She mirrored his position, shoulder to shoulder with him. The sky was streaked with purple now, and she enjoyed the stretch of heat down her side that his presence created as she stared up at it in wonder. "You suspect the apples are harmless, but how can you know for sure? Just because they were a gift from a titan doesn't mean they are safe for those who are not gods to consume. They could be like ambrosia, deadly to others than the gods."

He chuckled, then stood in one smooth motion. Spreading his wings, he lifted off the ground and flew to the top of the tree, plucking a perfect gold apple from the branches. He landed and offered it to her. "Would you like to know for yourself?"

Shocked, Medea stared at the forbidden fruit cradled in the nest of his fingers. The apple was the same color as his eyes. She pushed it away with both hands. "Are you mad?" she whispered. "Be rid of it!"

"It's fruit, Medea. Nothing more." A talon sprang from the first knuckle of his right hand, and he sliced through the peel. The inside was strange, segmented like no fruit she'd had before, not like an apple at all. He pulled it apart and popped a segment into his mouth.

Medea gasped. "What are you doing?"

"I've had it before. It's very good." He took another step closer. "I've told you, Medea, the rules don't apply to me. I can eat the sheep. I can eat the fruit. I can even leave the garden. The only question is, do you trust me enough to try it for yourself?"

He gave her a wicked smile that Medea thought must hold all the secrets of the universe. Her heart thudded in her throat. His gaze locked onto hers, and he held out a wedge, juice dripping from his fingers. Her throat turned dry as a stone. If she could just taste it, taste him... Was she really going to do this?

"But you are a dragon. An immortal! It may not hurt you, but what will it do to me?"

His eyes narrowed. "I don't understand exactly what you are Medea, but I know this fruit won't hurt you. Do you trust me?"

She searched her heart and found she did. Tentatively, she sat up and opened her mouth like a baby bird. He placed the fruit on her tongue. Sweetness burst across her taste buds, and she sucked the juice from his fingers, rolling the slice against her cheek. The taste wasn't metallic despite the gold outer appearance. It tasted like liquid sunshine. She closed her eyes and moaned as she chewed.

She opened them again when his lips met hers. The sweet fruit held no glory compared to the kiss. Swallowing, she gave herself over to the honeyed taste of his mouth melding with hers. If the fruit had any ill effects on her, she didn't feel them. All she knew was the heat of his touch and a strange mounting pleasure. A heaviness formed between her legs, a throbbing ache that she instinctually knew only he could soothe.

Her hands smoothed over his short hair, down his neck, and over his shoulders. He pulled her into his lap, his fingers stroking the thin fabric over her breast and toying with her nipple. He broke away from the kiss and bowed his head to suckle the tip. When he lifted his head again, the sensation was exquisite, the warmth of his tongue replaced by a delicious cool nip from the wet material.

She stared at him, breathless. "Tavyss, I..." She ran a hand down her body. "I ache for you."

He wrapped an arm around her and tangled his fingers in her hair, the long lashes of his eyelids lowering. The purr she'd heard him make before grew louder, and she placed her palm against his chest, feeling the vibration.

"*Mine.*"

"Your voice sounds strange."

His hand found the bare skin of her ankle and stroked up her calf to her knee. "Say you are mine, Medea. Be my mate."

His fingers explored higher, stroking along her inner thigh. She panted at the heat, the way the spot between her legs grew wet and ultrasensitive. She had the strongest urge to shift her hips against those fingers.

He squeezed her thigh and gripped the back of her hair. Medea's lips parted at the feeling. She wanted him. Everything she'd read in the strange forbidden book she'd conjured about sex, she wanted to try with him.

"Say you are mine," he demanded. "Be my mate."

"Mate..." She glanced away, confused at the term, but then she realized it was exactly as she'd hoped. He was asking her to wed him, to become a family as her mother and father were a family. "You wish me to become your wife? Be with you always?"

"I love you, Medea. Every part of me. The dragon and the man."

She took his face in her hands. "Yes, Tavyss. I will be your mate."

Mercifully, his hand crept to the tangle of nerves that throbbed between her legs and painted delectable circles there.

"Oh," she said, surprised by the sheer pleasure of it. It was far better than anything she'd imagined based on the book.

Clinging to him, she worked her hips, doing what instinctively made the pleasure more intense. The most marvelous magic unraveled from her lower belly, seizing her in a cascade of golden stars that arched her back and left her gasping for air. He held her as her body spasmed with the intensity of it.

Only when she'd come down from a great height did she remember the other things she'd read about. She reached for his breeches and untied them at the waist. Her hand brushed the long hard length of him. Would it truly fit inside her? She had her doubts.

"You're sure?" he asked. "My mate, once we do this, you will always be mine and I yours, until the moon crumbles into dust."

She thought of her sisters, of her family, for she knew to the core of her soul that this was no small promise she made to Tavyss. She was binding herself to him, the same way she was bound to them. No, in a much stronger way. She felt the magic, thick in the air around them, licking her skin.

But she was a woman, and she was ready for this. She wanted a full life like her parents had had, with a partner, maybe children of her own.

"Yes, Tavyss. I am yours."

Gently he leaned her back against the moss, her dress bunched around her hips, and settled between her legs. His breeches were gone, and he tugged his tunic over his head. Seeing him above her, a mass of dark golden power, almost flooded her body with pleasure again. She tugged her own dress over her head and cast it aside.

Allowing her knees to fall to the sides, she bared herself to him, reached for him. His wings unfurled, reflecting the moon gloriously in the twilight. With one flex, he was over her, blunt head parting her most sensitive flesh. Slowly, ever so slowly, he pushed inside. There was the slightest pressure, then pain, but she lost sight of it in the ever-building pleasure as he gently began to move.

Above her, his wings stretched gloriously. For weeks she'd longed to touch them, to see them up close. She stroked along the edge, trailing her fingers over the webbed flesh that stretched to his back. *Fascinating.* He shivered above her at her touch, and so she increased her ministrations, reveling in his reaction. Soon his rhythm grew more urgent. Gentle movements turned to firm thrusts.

She wrapped her arms and legs about him, longing for more. Only wanting to get closer to him. Only wanting him deeper inside her. The magic was back again, and this time she could hear in his trill that it had seized him as well. Power flooded her veins, radiating pure light as they both pitched over the edge.

Everything caught fire. The trees around her lit up with magical light as if they'd ignited a room full of candles. And all she could think was that something amazing had just happened. Something, judging by Tavyss's expression, he wasn't expecting.

CHAPTER TEN

W hen a dragon bonded with his mate, it was for life. There would be no other woman for Tavyss but Medea. He'd offered, and she'd consented. And although what they'd done had certainly sealed his fate, for him the connection was permanent the moment she'd accepted his offer.

But as the light faded and her breath came back to her in a gasp, Tavyss realized the danger he was in. Medea was most certainly powerful. The blast of power they'd given off was nothing short of celestial. That energy was far more than what he could put off on his own.

He stroked her hair back from her face and transferred his weight to the patch of moss beside her. Never taking his eyes off her, he asked, "Do you know what you are, Medea?"

Her gaze broke away from his for a fraction of a second, darting to the side. He didn't miss it. "I love you, Tavyss."

"I love you too. But now you must tell me the truth, the entire truth, of how you came to be here and how you wield such power."

Tears formed in her eyes, and his heart broke to see it. It

wasn't his intention to cause her pain, but he couldn't protect her if he didn't know the truth. His inner dragon chuffed at the thought. Yes, it was clear he'd need to protect her. If she was from the outside and therefore forbidden from living in the garden, that meant Hera could never know she was here.

"I wanted to tell you the truth. More than once, I tried and failed. I just couldn't. I... I was afraid you'd never speak to me again, or worse."

"But now you must tell me. There is nothing you can say that will turn me from you. I have already examined several scenarios in my mind. I am prepared. Tell me what you are."

In fact, he'd considered a range of possibilities. He'd guessed a witch but there were others. Perhaps she was a lesser goddess, hiding here from some sort of trauma, or a type of fairy from another land. That would explain the wings and the magic. He'd known extremely powerful fairies in his day.

"I am a witch," she said.

Tavyss sighed as the truth settled in. As he'd suspected. He closed his eyes against the pain of the revelation. "You lied. You were not born in the garden as you said?"

Her eyebrows rose toward her hairline. "I was born here," she insisted. "As were my sisters. I didn't lie about that. But I let you assume that meant we were creatures of the garden, and we are not. Our parents were from the outside."

"How?" He pulled back. In his home world of Paragon, dragons did not often consort with witches. A witch's magic was strange. While a dragon's flesh was inherently magical, lending to their talent for invisibility and for protecting their treasure, a witch could command the elements. Witches, most certainly, were not allowed in the Garden of the Hesperides.

"A long time ago, my parents performed a service for the Egyptian goddess Isis that involved them journeying into the underworld. When their work was done, the goddess hid them here so that they would be safe from the retribution of Hades for what they'd done. My mother was pregnant and gave birth to me and my sisters here in the garden."

"That's impossible. As an Egyptian goddess, Isis could not get past me or through the gates. Hera's own wards protect this garden, and my own ensure I'd never miss a soul trying. Hermes, I'd believe, or Zeus himself. But not Isis. It's impossible."

She sat up and tugged her dress over her head and down around her ankles. The neck fell over one shoulder in a way that made him long to take her in his arms again. It was dark now, but his dragon sight ensured he could see her clearly.

"My father sang you to sleep."

His eyes widened at the thought. Wouldn't he remember if something like that happened? "No."

"Yes. His name is Orpheus, and he is a descendant of the sorceress Medea, my namesake. He inherited a powerfully magical voice. Not only did his song soothe you to sleep, it wiped your memories of him and my mother."

Tavyss's fists clenched. Medea could not be held responsible for her parents' indiscretions, but the idea that Orpheus had used his sorcery to overpower him caused his throat to burn with pent-up rage.

"Even if he charmed me to sleep, he couldn't have made it through the enchantment in the gate. That was placed by Hera herself."

"That would be the work of my mother Alena. She is a descendant of Circe and a master of transfiguration. She transformed a worm into a key while it was in the lock. You see, the worm conforms—"

"I see." He didn't need it explained to him as if he were a child. He stood, swept his tunic from the ground, and began to dress.

"Tavyss, I'm sorry. I should have told you before."

"Yes, you should have. Your parents have broken the goddess's law. You are not to blame, and I will make it my mission to protect your place here, but Orpheus and Alena must be punished for their trespassing. Hera must be informed."

"No!" Medea scrambled to her feet. "She'll kill them. You can't tell her."

"I won't have a choice." He looked at her desperately. "When the goddess installed me as the Guardian at the Gate, she ensured that I could not lie to her. If she asks, I will have to answer truthfully."

"Then say nothing. Give her no reason to ask."

He glared at her, his wings snapping open with his burgeoning anger. "And let them get away with it?"

Medea recoiled as if he'd slapped her. "If they hadn't, I, your mate, would not be here. I would have never been born."

Her words sliced into his heart and made his breath hitch.

"What harm have we done, Tavyss? We've lived here our entire lives, and my parents and sisters have never touched a sheep or taken a bite of an apple until the one you fed me tonight. We live on fish, roots and berries—nothing forbidden. The nymphs have helped us from the beginning. We belong here. This is our home."

Tavyss heard the pleading in her voice, saw the tears forming in her eyes, and for a moment he wanted to comfort her. He longed to stroke her hair and tell her everything would be all right. Her wild-orchid scent grew stronger with her anger and fear. But there was an undeniable truth that he had sworn an oath to Hera. If he didn't fulfill his duty to the goddess, what did that say about him? Was he no better than his corrupt brother and sister, having no regard for duty or loyalty if it inconvenienced his will?

"You don't understand. I am bound—" Tavyss paused his pacing in front of her. A dark thought entered his mind. Her magic was strong, as strong as a god's. He grabbed her by the shoulders. "Where did you learn the spell you used to project me to Paragon?"

Her mouth dropped open, and he could see fear in her eyes. Good, she needed to be afraid. If it was what he thought it was…

"I learned it from our book of magic."

"Your book?" Relief washed over him. Maybe he was wrong. Maybe she'd learned everything she knew from her parents. "Your parents taught you everything you know? A family grimoire?"

She looked away. "Not my family's. Mine and my sister's. We needed to learn how to use our power, and ours is so different than our parents'. Our magic stems from our tree, you understand. The tanglewood tree. As Tanglewoods, we need to know how to wield the power we were born with; so we used our magic to conjure a teacher, and the book came to us."

Cold horror crept up his spine, and he gripped her elbows. His dragon was dangerously close to the surface, and he saw the glow of his eyes light up her face. "Show me the book, Medea."

With a shaking hand, she reached into her pocket and pulled out the gemstone. It was a diamond the size of a walnut, the same one she'd used to cast him into Paragon. At her suggestion, he held the stone up to his eye. He shouldn't be able to see a thing, not with only the light of a single moon to go by, but the grimoire inside the stone put off its own golden glow. There, contained within the facets of the stone, was a book with an ornate golden cover inscribed with a peacock. Shards of ice formed in his stomach as he turned the stone and watched the pages flip, expand, and come into focus.

Magic spells. A collection of charms and incantations designed by the gods themselves.

There could be no mistake. *This was Hera's golden grimoire!*

CHAPTER ELEVEN

Confusion pounded against the inside of Medea's skull until her head ached. She'd never seen Tavyss so furious. His skin roiled as if his inner dragon fought him for control. Talons sprang from the knuckles of his hand, and his eyes glowed gold in the darkness. If they hadn't just made love, she would have thought he wanted to kill her. Maybe he would kill her. She remembered the day she'd surprised him and he'd thrown her against the tree. He'd said he was a warrior. Her father had called him a furious beast. Was it possible she'd overestimated his capacity for compassion?

It was full dark now. Late. Her mother and father would be looking for her. Her sisters must be worried sick. But Medea dared not leave him now. Something was desperately wrong.

Tavyss backed away, shaking his head. "I have to return this to Hera. I'll find a way to do it that makes her assume it came from Paragon."

As quick as she could move, Medea drew her wand from her sleeve and uttered a retrieval spell. The gem flew from

167

Tavyss's hand into hers. "No, you will not! It's mine and my sisters'. You shall not take it. Not even for the goddess." She didn't know where she got the courage to defy him, because Tavyss in this state was terrifying.

He bared his teeth. "It's Hera's book, Medea. She won't rest until it is returned. She's charged me with recovering it." He held out a hand expectantly to her. "I won't be able to lie. If she finds out you have it, she will smite you from this world and the next."

Medea straightened. "And what gives her the right? She abandoned the book in the underworld. I retrieved it fairly with my own skill and resources. Isn't that the way of the gods and men? Did not Jason secure the golden fleece in the same such manner? And Hercules, the head of Medusa?" She watched him recoil. "We both know all the stories. Hers is not the only book we've conjured. My sisters and I are well studied in the ways of man."

He snatched her wrist and squeezed. The gem dropped into his opposite hand.

"Oww! You're *hurting* me!"

"I'm sorry, but it is my duty to return this to the goddess. I do this for us, Medea. She will not leave us alone without it."

"My sisters and I are still learning the limits of our magic. This is our guide. We use the book every day. You can't take it." She raised her wand, her body tensing with her growing ire.

"*She'll. Kill. You.*" Tavyss's ring radiated gold. The spell she cast bounced harmlessly off his shield.

Medea trembled with the awful emotions overwhelming her. "Tavyss, you can't possibly think that simply giving this back to Hera will stop her bitter tirade. She'll want to know where you found it, and then she'll come for me anyway."

Tavyss growled, his wings snapping out to their full glory. Would he shift into that dark and deadly dragon she'd seen outside the gates?

"Medea? Medea?" Orpheus's voice drifted out from the garden.

"That's my father. I have to go. *Please*, Tavyss. Don't give it back to her, not before we have time to talk again. Come back tomorrow please. Think about what you are doing!"

For a long moment, she stared at him, her heart breaking with disappointment. How could he even consider hurting her family? He simply shook his head. She could wait no more. Her father was close, and this was no time to make acquaintances. With one last pleading glance, she tucked her wand away and raced for home.

CHAPTER TWELVE

Tavyss landed in front of the stone cottage and barged through the door, the gem clutched in his hand. Rage glowed bright and hot in his chest, and he spit fire into the hearth, setting the logs ablaze. He paced the small room, blood burning, and watched the flames dance in the grate.

She'd played him for a fool! Even if she hadn't directly lied to him, she'd known she was misleading him. Had she realized all along he'd been searching for the grimoire when she'd cast him to Paragon? No, she couldn't have. He'd purposely not mentioned exactly what the goddess was looking for, wanting to spare her the details. Still, she'd taken the book without permission. She was a thief and a liar.

By the Mountain, she was his mate.

He ran a hand down his face. Flashes of her body under him filled his mind, what it felt like to bury himself deep between her thighs. Instantly his flesh responded to the memory. He was ready for her again. Wanted her again. Was desperate to have her here, to hold her tonight.

Fuck, what was he thinking? She couldn't live *here*. Now that he knew what she was, the safest place for her was in that garden where Hera's attention never strayed. The only other place she'd be safe from the goddess was on Paragon, and that destination would most assuredly not be safe for him.

He cursed. She'd have to continue living in the garden, but he could not be apart from her. Not now that they were mated. Perhaps he could build a cottage of their own next to the orchard. He couldn't shirk his duty guarding the gate, but they could have their own place, their own stolen moments.

Fuck, he wanted more than stolen moments. He wanted all of her moments.

He stormed toward the bed and tossed the gem onto the small table beside it. Stretching out on the lumpy mattress, he stared at it, wishing there was some way he could both appease the goddess and serve his mate. The worst part was, she was right. She'd won the book by her own merits, through cunning and magical strength, and by Hera's own admission, the goddess had not noticed it was gone. Hera admitted she hadn't looked for the book in decades, and Medea wasn't old enough to have taken it that long ago. Which meant that Hera didn't care about the book itself, only her pride and revenge.

A growl rumbled in his chest. Maybe he should return the book to Medea. Nothing about Hera was deserving. But then, that was a ridiculous, impossible idea. Hera would expect him to deliver the book. She was already obsessed. He could only put her off for so long. What he needed was to sleep. An idea would come to him in the morning.

He closed his eyes and slipped away, drawn into dreams of Medea, his mate.

❧

LIGHT AND HEAT FLOODED TAVYSS'S FACE. HAD MORNING come so soon? He'd spent the night tossing and turning, made restless by the decision before him. Now his eyes burned as he cracked them open.

"Hera!" The light that woke him was not the sun but radiated from the goddess who hovered over him.

"Good morning, dragon. You'll excuse the early visit, but I came as soon as I saw it in my looking glass. You found the book!"

She lifted the diamond from his bedside table and held it up toward the window. Never before had she called up the garden in her looking glass, but that did not mean she couldn't see his cottage. He was stupid not to have foreseen this turn of events.

"I told you to bring this to me immediately upon its retrieval. I trust you have reason for the delay."

He cleared his throat. "I don't know how to free it from the jewel."

She stared down her nose at him in quiet condescension. "I care not about the state of it. Only that it is back in my possession."

His head began to pound. "Why go through such trouble to get it back if you have no intention of using it?"

Her face morphed into a monstrous visage. "Because it's *mine*. I don't want it, but I don't want anyone else to have it." Her sleek blond eyebrow arched toward her hairline as she clenched her teeth. "You're a fool if you don't realize that this book in the wrong hands could be a weapon of mass destruction."

What was it Medea had said? Her parents had kept the book out of the wrong hands. That was how they ended up here to begin with, as a reward for saving the realm of men from this book. They'd proven themselves worthy of it but had selflessly let it go.

"What will you do with it now?" Tavyss asked quietly.

She shrugged as if it didn't matter one way or the other. "Return it to the protection of the underworld."

He frowned. How was that safe? The book had almost been retrieved by a tyrant and had been called up by an untrained sorceress. It was clear the goddess didn't care. She was already growing restless and easing toward the peacock feather.

"Leave it in my care," he blurted, an idea sparking somewhere in his aching brain.

She turned slowly back toward him, her eyes narrowing. "What are you talking about?"

"The book was stolen from the underworld to begin with. It's not safe. Dragons are experts at protecting their treasure. Leave it with me, and you'll never lose it again."

She paused, rolling the gem between her thumb and forefinger. "Strange that the book is sealed within a jewel. Paragon is known for its many jewels, is it not?"

He said nothing.

"And now you offer to guard this treasure. Where exactly did you find this, Tavyss?"

"I think you know where."

"Hmm. Yes. It must be Paragon. I can see everywhere else. It appeared in my looking glass quite suddenly last night, didn't it? Clearly when you arrived from your homeland."

He watched her slither around the room like a viper.

"The question is, where in Paragon did you find it?" She smiled wickedly. "Was it with your mate?"

He clenched his jaw and shook his head.

"Ahhh. You do wear your heart on your sleeve, dragon. You know she'll have to pay. No one steals from me and gets away with it."

He blinked slowly, his head beginning to pound. "You have your book. Just go."

She scanned him from head to toe, her eyes narrowing to slits. "All right," she said softly. Too softly. His body tensed, ready for anything. "For now."

She turned, touched the feather, and was gone.

Tavyss wasted no time seeking out Medea. He needed to tell her he'd been wrong. He needed to beg her forgiveness.

At first he couldn't find her, but then she appeared quite suddenly beside a clearing.

"Medea. I looked everywhere for you."

She scowled. "It's good to know the wards around the house are working. Perhaps I should disappear inside them again." She turned as if to leave.

"You've warded your home?" He should have known a witch would, but still the sophistication of the spell surprised him. She was undeniably powerful.

"Against supernatural creatures, yes. Shall we put it to the test?"

She took a step, and he picked up a slight shimmer in the air before her.

"No!" He held up his hands to her. "Medea, please. I need to speak with you."

"About what? About how you plan to bring about the certain death of my parents? How you plan to crawl on your knees back to a bitter, hateful goddess who cares nothing for anyone but herself?"

He shook his head. "No. I came to apologize. You were right. I shouldn't have taken the book from you."

All the tension drained from Medea's expression, her

softened features overflowing with relief. "Then you'll give it back?"

"I can't. Hera has it."

Medea blew out a breath as if he'd physically punched her, light dwindling from her eyes. Her disappointment was a bitter, palpable thing that made his bones turn to lead. He could almost smell her disgust.

"And I suppose she plans to seal it away somewhere." She scoffed.

"I—" Tavyss was about to admit he had no idea what Hera would do when a blinding light blasted between them, painful in its intensity.

He turned his face away and shielded his eyes. When he turned back, Hera was there, her teeth bared, her hands balled into fists. She unclenched her right hand to reveal the jewel that held the book nestled in her palm.

"What business is it of yours what I do with *my* book?"

Medea's skin was flushed from the blast of heat they'd endured, but her head didn't bend at all as she answered. "I won the book fairly. It is mine."

"Insolent girl!" Hera hissed. "Living in my garden without my permission, using my book, wooing *my* dragon." Fury rolled off the goddess in bright, hot waves, her body growing to seven... eight... nine feet tall.

"Hera..." Tavyss said, but the goddess was livid. He'd never get through to her.

"If you want the book so much, perhaps you belong in the underworld with it!" Hera snarled at Medea, raising her hands above her head as if to strike his mate.

Tavyss had often heard talk of Zeus and his lightning bolt, but he wondered why Hera's weapon wasn't similarly feared. A great ring of celestial fire appeared in her hand, its edges razor-sharp and molten red against the blue sky. Medea's expression morphed into terror as the goddess aimed for her head.

Tavyss's dragon tore from his body, transforming so quickly it felt as if he'd exploded from a shell. He'd placed his dragon scales between Hera and Medea before he even had time to consider if they'd be strong enough to withstand the goddess's power. Dragon scales were fireproof and laced with inherent magic, but Hera's weapon was charged with celestial fire. Would they stand the test?

The ring cracked against his scales. Searing pain radiated through him, but his scales held. Uninjured, he coiled and snapped, his teeth passing harmlessly through Hera's form. She reappeared a few yards away, her eyes wide in surprise.

"*Anaktó*," Medea called from behind him. The gem flew from Hera's hand and landed in her own. Her sisters were there, flanking her, wands drawn.

Hera's eyes flicked to his, the fire forming again in her hand. "You can't win this, dragon. You'll never defeat me in battle, and there is nowhere you can run that I can't go."

He growled, low and menacing, but even his dragon brain understood that only half of that statement was true. Hera released her ring of fire, hurling it at the three sisters with a vengeful hiss. Tavyss knocked it from the air, then swiped, his claws slashing through the goddess. In a flurry, he transformed back into his two-legged form and grabbed Medea's hand. Her sisters clung on, Circe to Medea's elbow and Isis to his own.

Tavyss's ring radiated gold light. He slashed an *x* through the air, opening a portal to Paragon even as Hera formed again, shrieking behind him. Heat from the goddess's weapon flamed against his back, but they had already stepped through to the world she was forbidden to inhabit. His feet touched down on rocky soil, and the portal closed quickly behind them.

EPILOGUE

Six months later...

T he day Tavyss had brought her to the world of Ouros, the land of the five kingdoms, Medea had believed the trip was temporary. After all, he'd explained to her that he'd abdicated the throne and that his siblings would murder him if he ever set foot in Paragon again. But Tavyss rightly warned that they could not return to the garden. Hera would likely be watching. And while they'd managed to get a message back to her parents using magic—they were well, thank the stars—she had no desire to call unnecessary attention to them living right under Hera's nose.

Fortunately, the kingdom of Paragon was only one of the five kingdoms of Ouros. All five fell under the protection of the goddess Aitna, the daughter of a titan whose affair with Zeus had bound her to this island realm. Once Isis, Circe, Tavyss, and she had discussed their options and the most likely places to take them in, they settled on Darnuith, the kingdom of the witches. Notoriously isolated, it was the perfect place for Tavyss to avoid detection by his siblings.

Darnuith was a mountainous territory, and Medea and her sisters had made a perilous journey to the capital city of Mistcraven. There they beseeched the leader of the coven, Queen Ferula, an ancient but powerful presence dressed in purple robes, fur, and bones, for a home among the witches. Queen Ferula's advisor, Zelaria, insisted she and her sisters perform a display of strength to prove their magic was strong enough to warrant a home among the witches. Together, the three sisters stopped the snow from falling, caused the sun to shine on the people of Mistcraven, and enchanted the clouds to perform a short, silent play in the sky above about a turtle who fell in love with a fish.

"And what of you, dragon," the queen had asked Tavyss. "Can you serve your kingdom and Darnuith?"

"I have no intention to serve Paragon, my queen. I am mated to Medea. My service and protection belong to her and her people."

"Hmm." Queen Ferula tapped her chin. "A dragon is a powerful gift indeed."

"My queen, we do not know—" Zelaria began, but Ferula cut her off with a dismissive wave.

"You are welcome to stay. You will take over the Fatsed Orchard. The wizard has passed away, and we've had no fruit since his death. Make the trees grow and you'll be welcome here always."

"It would be our pleasure," Medea said.

"There is only one thing. It is our custom, for our citizens to have a surname. I am Ferula Northstar. What name shall you take as your second?"

Medea thought for a moment, her gaze drifting to her sisters. "Tanglewood, my queen."

Ferula gave a crooked grin. "Hmm. Fitting. Welcome Medea Tanglewood."

They'd moved into a simple cottage, and through the steady use of magic brought to life peaches, apples, bon bon fruit, and the most delicious figs Medea had ever tasted. And then, in a feat of magic she wasn't at all sure would work, each of the three sisters clipped a segment off the end of their wands and planted the pieces in a common hole. Watered with blessed rain and fed with their own blood, the pieces rooted and grew into a new tanglewood tree.

At night she'd lay next to Tavyss and drift to sleep, blissfully tired from a day of meaningful farming.

"Do you regret becoming my mate?" he asked her one night. The solemnness in his tone made her lift her head from his chest to look him in the eye.

"Not for a moment. I think my life began the day you flew over that pool in the garden."

"I know mine did."

"There is one thing that could make me happier." She smiled at him in the darkness. They'd made love then, both opening themselves to the potential for a baby.

As the days rolled by, even her sisters seemed happy. Circe was slaking her thirst for botanical knowledge by learning what she could from an apothecary in the village, and Isis had found friendship with a team of hunters who frequented the ice forest on the east coast of Darnuith.

All was well for a time.

But then one day everything changed.

"Medea? Medea, come quickly." Circe ran through the orchard toward her, waving her hands. Her eyes were swollen and red from crying.

"What's wrong, sister?"

"It's Queen Ferula. She's passing into the next world. She's called all witches to her side. There's a ceremony—

some ancient ritual they perform to pick her successor before she dies."

As if he sensed her distress, Tavyss flew to Medea's side from where he'd been harvesting fruit. "What is happening?"

Circe brought him up to speed.

Tavyss took on a far-off look. Medea had seen that expression before when he was thinking about the past or his childhood. "It's called the Sacred Lots. The witches of Darnuith ask the Fates to bless the next queen. It is a solemn ritual. It would be rude not to attend."

Medea tucked her wand into her sleeve and helped him ready the horses. Together with Circe, they journeyed to the temple at the heart of Mistcraven, called Maelhaven.

Red wooden pillars stretched three stories toward a clay roof. Medea had never been inside the golden doors of Maelhaven—only the queen was allowed inside the heart of the sacred space—but even in the courtyard, the place made her feel both small and significant, as if she were part of a greater magic than herself.

Today the queen lay on a settee at the center of the square, skin tinted with a gray pallor, eyes rheumy and distant. Her breath came in tiny, barely detectable sips.

Tavyss rubbed Medea's shoulders supportively as they joined the back of the massive crowd. Every witch in Darnuith was there as far as Medea could tell. They gathered in rings around the dying woman.

A few minutes later, Isis arrived, still dressed in her hunting garb. "I heard the horns. Is it true? Ferula is dying?"

"It appears so," Medea said. She hadn't known the queen well and observed the proceedings with a measure of detachment.

"Has she been ill?" Circe asked.

An elderly man in front of them turned around to address Circe's question. "She is two hundred years old, only held together by alchemy. It is her time."

At the center of the crowd, Zelaria passed her staff over a giant cauldron in front of the settee. At her prompting, the crowd began to move, circling in front of the queen, each witch, young and old, male and female, reaching inside.

"What is this?" Medea asked. "What do we do?"

"Take a stone from the cauldron. If the Fates choose you, it will change color and Ferula will say your name with her last breath," Tavyss explained.

"But we're new. Only here six months. Surely we don't participate."

The elderly man faced them again and pointed a gnarled finger at her. "All citizens must participate. Everyone with magic. If you don't, the spell may not work."

Medea frowned. It seemed wrong to participate given her overall lack of experience with the kingdom.

"Don't concern yourself," Tavyss said. "Zelaria has trained by Ferula's side for decades and made sacrifices to the Fates. If things go as they have in the past, she will be named. That is how has always been. The ritual is more of a rite of passage." He gave her a reassuring nod.

They filed in behind the other witches, shuffling patiently as stone after stone was selected from the cauldron, each only as big as her thumb and as smooth as glass. They all looked the same.

After an hour, her legs began to ache and she squeezed Tavyss's hand. Circe exchanged glances with her and Isis, then produced a root from the pouch on her hip and split it between them. At once, Medea's energy returned and the pain in her legs faded.

Hours more had passed before they finally reached the

cauldron. She selected a smooth silver stone from the bottom and tucked its cold shape into her palm. Beside her, Ferula lay absolutely still, eyes closed, her breath barely discernible. Was she truly waiting to die until the ritual was complete?

Heart heavy, Medea followed the line away from the queen and returned to her place at the back of the crowd.

Tavyss must have noticed her exhaustion because he wrapped a comforting arm around her shoulders and kissed the side of her head. "It will be over soon."

With every stone selected, the crowd seemed to slip deeper into an atmosphere of solemnity. Not a word was spoken, not even in a whisper. The only sound was a large black bird with a strange hooked beak that circled overhead, cawing in a way that sounded like a cry. Medea watched its flight against the gray sky and wondered if it was a harbinger of death.

Finally all the stones were gone but one. Zelaria selected the last stone and held it toward the sky, whispering an incantation whose words Medea could not understand. All at once, the crowd raised their stones.

Medea did the same, although she fought the urge to drop it because hers had grown quite hot between her fingers. She thought it must be the magic and held on despite the discomfort.

Then, in the quiet, she heard the queen speak. "Medea."

That couldn't be right. Had she just said...? She looked at the ancient woman in confusion.

"Medea," the queen repeated, her voice weak but carrying, whatever magic was at work amplifying its natural volume.

A murmur traveled through the crowd as people opened

their hands and checked their stones. Who was Medea? The few who knew her turned to stare in her direction.

"Medea, your stone." Tavyss grabbed her wrist and thrust her hand toward the sky.

Blue light shone between her fingers and blasted outward as if she were holding a star.

Isis swore and Circe clamped a hand over her mouth. There was a gasp as the witches around her noticed and, one by one, dropped to their knees.

"No," Medea whispered. "This can't be right."

Her gaze snapped to Ferula, whose eyes were open now and locked with hers. The queen's mouth stretched into a smile.

"Medea," she whispered one more time before her body turned to dust and blew away on the wind.

Zelaria's eyes locked onto hers, the advisor's face a mask of confusion and some other well-hidden emotion. She gave Medea a tiny, practiced bow.

Hundreds of faces looked up at her expectantly.

With a sharp tap of her staff, Zelaria announced in a strained and shaky voice, "Blessed be, Medea Tanglewood, witch queen of Darnuith!"

❦

Thank you for reading the Tanglewood Witches. If you enjoyed this title, please leave a review wherever you purchased this book.

Medea has found herself in the unenviable position of being named queen to a strange kingdom barely known to her. Will she rise to the occasion? And will becoming royalty in the five kingdoms make it impossible to hide her mating to Tavyss, the true and rightful heir to the kingdom of Paragon?

Find out in Tanglewood Magic, the next novella in the Three Sisters Trilogy!

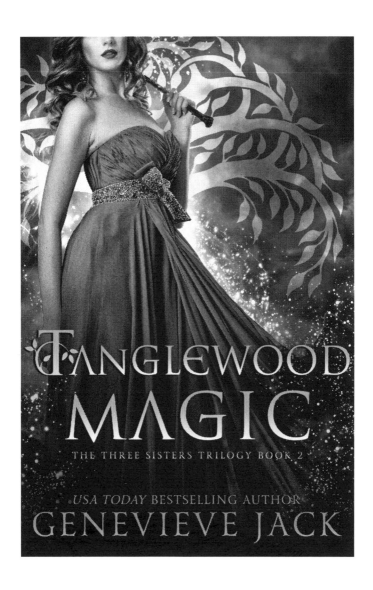

TANGLEWOOD
MAGIC

THE THREE SISTERS TRILOGY BOOK 2

USA TODAY BESTSELLING AUTHOR
GENEVIEVE JACK

MEET GENEVIEVE JACK

Award winning and USA Today bestselling author Genevieve Jack writes wild, witty, and wicked-hot paranormal romance and fantasy. Coffee and wine are her biofuel. The love lives of witches, shifters, and vampires are her favorite topic of conversation. She harbors a passion for old cemeteries and ghost tours, thanks to her years attending a high school rumored to be haunted. Her perfect day involves a heavy dose of nature and one crazy dog. Learn more at GenevieveJack.com.

Do you know Jack? Keep in touch to stay in the know about new releases, sales, and giveaways.

Join my VIP reader group
Sign up for my newsletter

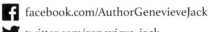

facebook.com/AuthorGenevieveJack

twitter.com/genevieve_jack

instagram.com/authorgenevievejack

bookbub.com/authors/genevieve-jack

Made in United States
Orlando, FL
08 December 2021

11278118R00117